ALSO

Cedar Creek

Christmas at Cedar Creek

Snowstorm at Cedar Creek

Pine Harbor

Allison's Pine Harbor Summer

Evelyn's Pine Harbor Autumn

Lydia's Pine Harbor Christmas

Holiday House

The Christmas Cabin

The Winter Lodge

The Lighthouse

The Christmas Castle

The Beach House

The Christmas Tree Inn

The Holiday Hideaway

Highland Passage

Highland Passage

Knight Errant

Lost Bride

Highland Soldiers

The Enemy

The Betrayal

The Return

The Wanderer

Highland Vow

American Hearts

Secret Hearts

Runaway Hearts

Forbidden Hearts

For more information, visit jljarvis.com.

CHRISTMAS AT CEDAR CREEK

CHRISTMAS AT CEDAR CREEK

J.L. JARVIS

CHRISTMAS AT CEDAR CREEK

Published by Bookbinder Press
bookbinderpress.com

ISBN (paperback) 978-1-942767-40-4
ISBN (ebook) 978-1-942767-39-8

"So, been on any good dates lately?" Matt Furnell didn't miss a beat as he shoveled potatoes onto his Thanksgiving dinner plate.

Sophie shot a pointed look at her brother. *Twenty-three on the outside and still thirteen on the inside.* She took a cleansing breath, smiled, and answered pleasantly. "Why, no, Matt, I haven't. Unlike you, I'm holding out for a date with opposable thumbs."

Unfazed, their parents exchanged glances and continued to eat.

Matt's eyes crinkled. "Okay, but seriously..."

"A girl's got to have standards."

Matt's eyebrows drew together. "Standards or roadblocks?"

Sophie decided to cut to the chase. "I've been busy."

With a nod, Matt said, "That's right. You're focusing on your career."

Sophie slowly blinked and said under her breath, "I would if I still had one."

Their mother gave Matt an admonishing look. "It's Thanksgiving. Let's have a nice dinner." She turned to her husband. "This deep-fried turkey is delicious!"

Now confused, Matt stared at Sophie. "What?"

Softly, she said, "I lost my job."

His jaw fell open. "Oh, crap. I'm sorry. What happened?"

With that, her brother showed signs of maturing, which only made sense since he was two years older than Sophie. It was bound to happen sometime. He looked sincerely remorseful, so she said, "Forget it."

"How? I thought you were doing so well."

"I thought I was too. But the mayor defunded the police, and the 911 call center went with it. I mean, it's still there, but I'm not. I guess I should've seen it coming the night I had to tell a woman help was not on the way. There was no one available. She'd just gotten home from the hospital, and her ex-boyfriend was pounding on her front door threatening to finish the job." Sophie swallowed. "All I could think of to tell her was to call a friend or a neighbor." Emotions threatened to overwhelm her, but she took a deep breath and pulled it together. "Anyway, last hired, first fired. I didn't make the cut."

"I'm sorry, Soph. Really."

She shrugged. "It is what it is." And what it was sucked. But she tried to appear philosophical. She didn't feel that way. She felt gutted and angry. But philosophical was a better look for her, especially now. She didn't want to be a holiday buzzkill. But in truth, she resented the move. People had called because they needed help, and she'd given it to them. Her work had changed lives, sometimes saved them, and that gave her life purpose. Used to give her life purpose. *Now what?*

Sophie's father cleared his throat. "Yeah, that deep fryer is something else. Turkey comes out nice and moist."

Her mother's eyes widened. "And I love how it freed up the oven!"

Sophie ignored her brother while he wallowed in well-deserved guilt. A lifetime of competitive banter should have taught him how these things usually ended—with Matt one step over the line and Sophie with the thrill of victory and no one to share it with.

By the time the meal ended, they'd found their way back to normal, "normal" being a relative term.

Then they moved on to the football portion of the day, where life was as it should be, at least for the time being. Tomorrow, Sophie would begin taking action to reassemble the pieces of her life. However, before the rebuilding could begin, she needed to finish tearing it down. No job meant no rent money, so she was due out of her apartment by the end of the month. At least she didn't have a car payment. Instead, she had Old Faithful, which had been proving itself to be not quite so faithful of late. The poor old all-wheel-drive hatchback had one hundred twenty thousand miles on it. She only hoped it would get her to her next job before it wheezed and sputtered its last carbon monoxide fumes into the ozone.

She was packing up books when the phone rang. "Grandma Kate! Hi! How are you?"

"I'm fine. I'm enjoying the lanai while I catch up on some reading. How are you?"

Sophie looked around at the stacks of boxes filling her apartment. "I'm great."

"No, you're not."

Sophie's bright mood vanished. "Mom told you."

"No, Matt did."

Sophie wasn't sure whether to gasp or say, "Aw." It wasn't Matt's place to tell Grandma Kate, but he wouldn't have done so if he didn't care. He did love her. But that meant he was worried about her, which meant there was reason to worry.

"Matt said you were moving."

"That's right. In fact, I'm surrounded by boxes at the moment."

"Where to?"

Good question. "I've hired a local company."

"Good start."

"And I've rented a storage unit."

"Very smart." That was so Grandma Kate, so full of confidence to make up for what Sophie lacked. "That buys you some time to find your best options and make good decisions."

I guess. I just needed a place for my stuff. "Well, I wasn't thinking about that exactly. It was more an act of desperation."

She could almost see her grandmother smiling. "That works too."

"Yeah, so I'm storing everything but my clothes, and I'm moving back home."

"Oh. Can you fit a bed in your old bedroom?"

"Well, no. I mean, Mom offered to make room, but I couldn't kick her out after she worked so hard to fix it up just how she wanted it. So I guess I'll move into the basement."

"Oh. Did they finish out their basement?"

"No, but all it needs is a throw rug, a lamp, and a brightly colored bedspread."

"Won't the noise of the sump pump keep you up nights?"

Sophie grimaced but said cheerily, "I'm a sound sleeper."

"Sophie." She could almost hear Grandma Kate shaking her head. "I just got off the phone with the Realtor. She's sending a cleaning crew over to spruce up my rental cabin."

"That's nice." *And also a quick change of subject. I guess my problems are kind of boring.*

Grandma Kate continued. "So it'll be all ready for you by the end of the week if you need someplace to stay. It sits empty for most of the off-season. You'd be doing me a favor if you'd house-sit. And if you're still there in the summer, we could work something out for the rent."

"Grandma." Sophie swallowed back her emotions. "Thank you. That would be..."

"Good. Then it's settled."

"Thank you!"

"Shh. Just relax. Take some time to regroup."

"I will. Thank you, Grandma."

"Don't be silly. Oh! Look at the time! I've got a tee time in a half hour. I'll send you the real estate agent's info, and you can always ask the neighbors next door if you need anything."

"I love you, Grandma!"

"Love you too. Bye, honey."

Grandma. Sophie shook her head. *And Matt!* Her life might be crumbling around her, but her family was looking out for her.

A week later, Sophie packed up her car and headed up to the mountains. She had made it through Thanksgiving and hadn't cried once. *I may have lost my job, but I've still got my dignity.*

As a tear trailed down her cheek, she took a deep breath, dabbed her eyes with her sleeve, and drove on. "That's okay. Everything's fine. Who needs a job when I can live on unemployment at Grandma Kate's cabin?"

She was one of the lucky ones. While her budget was tight, she wasn't desperate for cash. She had a rent-free place to stay and enough unemployment compensation for food, gas, and utilities. She hoped her family wouldn't mind homemade Christmas presents this year, because that was what they would be getting. Now all she had to do was find a way to set aside the overwhelming sense of abject failure at finding herself unemployed. Forget setting goals, mapping out a career, or managing her money. None of that was happening now. But thanks to Grandma Kate, she would get by. But she worried about the people she used to serve. Who would answer their calls? How long would it take for someone to get there?

Sophie stopped herself. *That's beyond my control.*

She drew in a deep breath and turned on the car stereo. *What I need is some Christmas!*

2

One week later

Standing in front of his bicycle shop, Cole Marick recalled better times. He loved the sport, and he knew its equipment. Since his college days in the city, he'd dreamed of owning a shop like this. Through hard work, he'd built it from a go-to place for serious cyclists to get proper repairs to a store carrying premier bicycles, parts, and accessories. He loved what he did and was proud of what he had accomplished. Now his store stood broken and covered in plywood, along with the rest of the shops on the street. Building it had taken years. Destroying it had taken only minutes.

Cole and his employees had defended the business until a street sign crashed through the storefront window, and a crowd of looters had poured in. That was the last thing Cole remembered. He'd woken in a hospital with two broken arms and a skull fracture where he'd been struck by something a lot harder than his head. If it hadn't been for his two employees dragging him through the back exit, he might not have survived. With no ambulance able to get through, they'd half-carried, half-dragged him ten blocks to the hospital.

In the weeks after his release from the hospital, while he lay recovering from his injuries, his stalwart employees had cleaned up the crumbled shell of a store and boarded up the front windows and door. When he was able to return to the site, a few of his neighbors had hoped to reopen their businesses, but most of them simply could not. Insurance covered most of the physical damage, but their business inter-ruption insurance had already run out. Customers weren't coming back. With no income, they just couldn't make it.

Cole made a decision. Physically, he had recov-ered, but even if he could get by financially for the months—or possibly years—it would take for the neighborhood to come back to life, he couldn't bring himself to do it. He couldn't let go of the thought that if it had happened once, it could happen again.

Interacting with people troubled him most. He

couldn't shake a nagging apprehension at the thought of customers coming into his shop. He'd spent weeks considering his options. Reopening made the most sense. God knew he'd tried to get used to the idea. But one of his last thoughts before he lost consciousness had been the sight of his attackers. They looked like his neighbors, no different from the people he passed every day on the street. They might have stood beside him in a grocery store line or sat beside him at the movies, which meant anyone he came into contact with was potentially capable of attacking him. It was impossible to imagine returning to live and work among people who had destroyed their own neighborhood.

They were more than just customers. He'd thought of them as neighbors and friends—all part of a community, living and working together to build and maintain a sort of hometown within the big city. But now, he would never see them in the same way again. Every time someone came into his shop, he would wonder if they had been there that night. If a group of people walked through the door, could he trust them not to turn hostile and knock him unconscious and loot his store all over again?

Cole had tried to overcome his fear with logic. He had taken a couple of psychology classes in college. He recalled studying how, in the heightened excitement of a crowd, individuals could abandon their sense of responsibility and adopt behaviors they would never have chosen on their own. Cole also recalled how he'd felt when they'd kicked him. And he remembered the glass. Time had seemed to slow to a stop as shattered pieces of store window flew like fractured bits of his life through the air. Like his dreams, they'd settled in a scattered and useless array.

The experience had changed how Cole viewed the world. From now on, he would see two types of people: builders and destroyers. With their mission accomplished, the destroyers could live with the fruits of their labor. As for Cole, he would go upstate to the family cabin and build a new life far from the madness overtaking the city.

His family still lived outside of Syracuse in a suburb surrounded by rolling farmland. But they owned an old fishing camp in the High Peaks region of the Adirondacks, and that was where he would live. When Cole was a boy, his father had taken him and his brother there to fish. It was rough, with no power or outhouse and a hand pump at the sink that drew water from the creek that ran past the back of the cabin. At night, they would sit outside around a campfire and talk about where they might hike or fish the next day. When it rained, they would build a fire in the fireplace and play cards and board games at the kitchen table by the light of the kerosene lantern. They were good memories of a simpler time, but the cabin and land hadn't changed. Only the towering cedars marked the years that had passed.

Cole had earmarked a small portion of the insurance settlement to put toward some modern improvements to the cabin. He would enjoy the luxury of an indoor toilet, for starters. He wouldn't mind some basic electricity, either. A generator would be enough to get by with until he could afford a solar array. As isolated as it was, the property was only a few miles off the main road. With a few scattered cottages nearby, there would be neighbors to look out for one another. This was a place he could live and be content.

If worse came to worst and the anarchists took over the country, he could try to sneak over the border to Canada. He laughed to himself. He didn't mean it. Still, there was no point in ruling it out as an option.

Cole traveled light. Everything that he needed fit into the back of his pickup. So he packed up and covered it all with a tarp, then set off for a quick stop at home on his way to the cabin. The streets were quiet, as though the riots of summer had never been meant to last more than a season. Now the lifeless leaves lay on the ground, with no purpose except to be tossed here and there by an occasional breeze.

As Cole drove out of the city, he reveled in the freedom of having no aim in life other than to reach his destination at no particular time. He stopped home for some lunch with his parents, then, leaving fast-food and convenience stores in his wake, drove on to the cabin. As he neared his new home, the familiar sights and the scent in the air brought memories of childhood contentment to the surface. Cole drove into the state park, where scattered leaves gripped bare branches and the air smelled of autumn and distant fireplace smoke.

Pulling off the main road, he followed a narrow country road that wound through the woods along-side Cedar Creek, which was high in its banks thanks to a recent snowfall now melting. Cole slammed his foot on the brakes as a deer leaped across the road. He slowed down. If there was one, more would likely follow. He smiled as two more deer followed and disappeared into the woods. For the next mile, he saw no signs of people, only the road and a few scattered houses. Cole was alone. There was something serene about seeing nothing but trees and smelling nothing but the earth and fallen leaves still clinging to remnants of snow.

He had made the right move. This was a soul-cleansing place. All his wounds, physical and emotional, would heal here.

He passed a couple of houses, then there it was: 17 Cedar Creek Road. He was home. Remnants of gravel long since indented by tires lined with a row of grass in the middle marked the driveway. *Cabin* might have been a generous term. It was more of a camp that backed up to the creek. Tall trees overshadowed the structure whose finest feature was a bold fieldstone chimney that stood out proudly among the stacked logs as though supporting its lesser relations. A half-caved-in outhouse stood off to the side, a remnant of the good old days that must have been great when nature called in the middle of the night. He resolved to put in a septic system before winter set in. To make it through the winter, he would need a wood-burning stove. Internet access was way down on the list of necessities, but he wouldn't mind some satellite access. Once he had all that in place, months in the snow-covered woods sounded perfect.

He got out of the car, took a few steps toward the door, and stopped. *What the heck? Singing?* To his left, on the same side of the creek as his camp, was a storybook cobblestone cottage dusted with snow. He remembered the cottage, but the young woman sweeping snow from its deck was not part of that memory. With an old straw broom for a partner, she was engaged in full-throated song.

"Great. I live next to frigging Snow White." Cole

braced himself, half expecting the birds to start chirping and carrying cedar garlands and fairy light strings in their beaks. Would every morning begin with strains of song cutting through his pristine wood-land tranquility? He could already imagine fishing season, when his beloved brook trout would head upstream like salmon, just to escape the show tunes.

No, she wasn't dancing, was she? Yes, she was. Then his new neighbor's dulcet tones turned to a cry. "Wha—oh—oof!"

Snow White slipped and fell to the deck.

3

Her eyes were open. That was a good sign—or a bad one if they stayed that way. He bent down. "Are you okay?"

She looked up at him. "Yeah. I'm fine. I just tripped."

"So I noticed." He hesitated, unsure of what to do next. She seemed perfectly lucid, yet immobile. He extended his hand. "Here, let me help you up."

She started to push herself up but, wincing, gave up. "No, that's okay. I just need a minute." She shooed him away with a wave of her hand. "Go ahead. I'll be fine."

"You don't look fine. I should call 911." He patted the pocket where he kept his phone, but it was empty. "I left my phone in the car. I'll have to use yours."

"Good luck getting a signal." She stirred a little. "I can still feel my toes." She wiggled her fingers. "Do you see any blood?"

"No."

"Can you see from up there?"

He knelt down for a closer look. "Nope, no blood, but you're flat on your back. I'm no doctor, but that can't be good. Where's your phone?"

She winced and sat up. "See? I'm up, and I'm fine."

"If you say so."

She extended her hand. "Sophie Furnell."

Cole tried not to smile at the contrast between her formal demeanor and her current state, seated unceremoniously on her snow-covered deck. He couldn't remember the last time he'd smiled. "Cole Marick." They shook hands.

Sophie reached for a chair for support. "I just need to get up."

Cole lurched forward and managed to get an arm around her back to pull her to her feet.

"That was easy." She made a face since it clearly was not. Once standing, she moved her arms then her legs. "Everything still seems to work. Looks like I'll live."

"Glad to hear it. But you might have to put your dancing career on hold."

She suddenly frowned. "Oh. You saw me dancing?"

Cole suppressed a smile.

"Yeah, well. I'm usually alone out here in the wilderness."

"Hey, don't let me cramp your style."

"I'm much better in a large room with a mirror—or I was when I was twelve. I guess I'm a little out of practice." A bashful smile lit her eyes. "Anyway, thanks for coming to my rescue."

"I wouldn't call it a rescue, but you're welcome." Their gazes lingered for a moment, until their smiles started to fade. Cole looked away. "I'd better go. I've got some unpacking to do."

"Right. Thanks again." She had an easy smile and bright, honest eyes.

"No problem." He smiled and went back to his cabin. Only then did he take a good look at his home. At first glance, it had all the charm he remembered. The second glance was the problem, though. It contained all the elements one could want in a woodsy fishing retreat. The metal roof, with its weathered patina, and the live-edged cedar siding that he'd always loved seemed to slope toward the creek. That would need to be jacked and leveled, but it should be doable. Then he stepped onto the porch. A plank sagged and cracked under his feet. As he righted himself, the graying window screens waved in the breeze. Cole made a mental note. Replacing a few rotten floorboards and tattered screens would be easy enough. He didn't mind digging into some projects.

The inside was a time capsule from the 1970s, complete with floral upholstery in faded autumn tones, a kitchenette with Formica countertops edged with aluminum strips, and the lingering odor of woodland roommates. *No worries.* That was the perfect sort of work to keep him from obsessing over his life, which had fallen apart, not unlike this cabin. But when he was done, he would have a home.

Sophie sat, phone in hand, with her feet propped up and an old gym sock filled with microwaved rice at her back. "No, I'm fine. I'm a little achy, but I'll live."

Matt said, "So, tell me more about the guy from next door. Is he an ax murderer?"

"No!"

"But, really, Soph, how can you tell?"

"Well, for one thing, he didn't have an ax."

"Well, phew. That's a relief!"

"I know! Isn't it?" She adjusted her homemade heating pad and repositioned herself. "So, Matt, why did you call?"

"Oh, just checking."

"On me?"

"Well, yeah."

"Aww!"

"No big deal. Mom made me."

Sophie smiled. "You know, Matt? You're a pain in the ass, but I don't entirely loathe you."

"Thanks. I love you too."

"And why wouldn't you? Now go do something productive that doesn't involve a game controller."

"How do you do that?"

"What, live without gaming?"

"No, read my mind."

Sophie rolled her eyes. "It's like a cheap novel. Plus, I heard your game's intro music in the background. Go play."

"Okay, bye. And lay off the ballet."

"Yeah, I might switch to tap."

"Oh, man. I just had a traumatic flashback of hearing you practice your flap-ball-change on the kitchen tile floor."

Sophie laughed. "Those were some good times."

"Yeah, something like that."

"Hey, Matt?"

"Yeah?"

"Thanks for calling."

"Yeah, whatever. See you!"

"Bye." She smiled and set down her phone, looking through the square windowpanes at the babbling brook. She'd had a slight setback with her job and her embarrassing dance fall, but she had family members looking out for her. Regardless of what had prompted her visit, it felt good to be here. It was Christmas. The nostalgic memories of childhood visits with her grandparents blended with the magical joy of the season. If those warm, fuzzy feelings didn't drive away all of her hopes and fears for all the years, she could always pull out the stops with some cookies, cocoa, and holiday movies. She drew in a breath filled with the scent of the simmering nutmeg, cloves, and cinnamon warming on the stove. *Mm, homemade cookies would hit the spot nicely!* She would get right on that immediately.

Cole finished unpacking and went to the back porch. A fly buzzed somewhere overhead. He pulled out his phone and started a punch list—new screens, exterminator, foundation, and rotting floorboards. Then he opened the creaky screen door to the yard and walked down to the water. He could almost feel his eight-year-old self brimming with delight as, fishing pole and tackle in hand, he would run to the edge of the creek and wait there for his father to catch up. His house might have been in the city, but the cabin was where he felt at home.

4

Morning sun washed the breakfast room while the aroma of freshly ground coffee wafted from the kitchen. Sophie winced as she added a log to the fire in the woodstove. She was sore from her fall, but not too much to finish her Christmas decorating. First, she needed some coffee.

She sat at the table by the window and looked out at the creek. *Thank you, Grandma.* The cottage had always held warm memories for her, but now it was her happy place—or it would be as soon as she could put her 911 call center memories behind her. She couldn't take it to heart. There were people who might not get the help they needed, but she'd done all she could do. Now she had to let go. That was what this respite from real life was meant for. Real-world troubles couldn't reach her up here. If she just blocked them out, she would be fine.

It was Christmas. She'd always been happy at Christmas, so she would be happy now—or later—but not too much later.

She caught sight of her neighbor down by the creek, standing ankle deep in the snow. Fresh snow weighed down the tree limbs. Every so often, a white clump would fall to the ground. That, along with the rushing creek water, would be one of the few sounds he would hear out there. She knew because she had stood by the creek more than once. She was tempted to join him but had to resist. Something about him warned her to stay at arm's length. He hadn't been unkind or rude. In fact, he had practically leaped over her deck rail to make sure she was all right. That was the act of a man who was inherently kind. But Sophie got the distinct sense that he'd come here to be alone, so she would respect that.

Not everyone loved her enthusiasm. She had a slight tendency to overcompensate when she was down. That was why she'd been singing. The dancing part hadn't worked out so well, but that was okay. She would find something safer to lift her spirits. *Hot chocolate!* She headed straight for the kitchen.

Cole made a mental list of supplies he would need for winter fly fishing. *A rod and reel might be a good start, and some midge flies.* If he went to town today, he would be geared up for midday fly fishing tomorrow. He watched the icy water rush over the rocks, despite the thin shelves of ice lining the banks. He hadn't realized he had missed this, but now he wondered how he'd stayed away. Cedar Creek would bring him back into balance. He couldn't feel anxious around people if there weren't any here. The only house in sight was his next-door neighbor's, and Sophie seemed harmless enough. She was better than harmless. She was a little quirky, but he liked her.

He barely minded her happy-puppy demeanor—as long as she kept her distance from him. He wasn't ready to start sharing cups of sugar or chatting over the back fence, if they'd had one. But there was something about her he hadn't seen in a long while. She was honest and unguarded. He found that refreshing. He just hoped, for her sake, she would learn to erect a few walls for protection. There were people in the world who took advantage of people like that. He would hate to see her get hurt.

With a quick look at his watch, Cole headed back to the cabin then grabbed his phone and car keys. He had some work to do on the cabin before he could reward himself with fishing. The first stop was the hardware store. When he got to his truck, Sophie's car was gone. He wondered where she'd gone—not that it mattered. It was just an idle observation. *It's normal to wonder.*

The clerk at the hardware store gave him the names of two contractors who could coordinate the work Cole couldn't do. After loading his new tools and supplies into his truck, he went to a small diner to grab a bite and call the contractors. He sat near the window so he could keep an eye on his truck. Small town or not, he wasn't taking any chances with the tools and materials he'd just bought lying unprotected in his truck bed.

His food came, and he gazed out the window as people walked by. No one looked stressed or late for an appointment. They smiled, said hello to each other, and sometimes stopped to chat. Cedar Creek was just as he remembered it. He might have fallen through time and landed here. He wouldn't really have minded.

His neighbor walked past the window. Sophie didn't see him. He felt a slight pang of disappointment that she hadn't, then he wondered where that had come from. He'd barely met her. They'd spent all of five minutes together, and yet he was drawn to her.

That was not part of the plan. He'd come here to be alone and recover. His physical wounds had healed, but he needed to work out some emotional issues. This attraction to Sophie was merely a symptom of adjusting to being alone. He wasn't used to it yet, but he would be soon enough.

To distract himself from his thoughts, he dialed the first contractor on his list, who gave him disappointing news. It was too cold to install a septic system or plumbing. That would best be left until spring. In the meantime, though, he could set Cole up with a composting toilet, which sounded more like a cat litter box. Still, it was better than an outhouse in subzero weather. On the plus side, he could have an electric pump installed for the sink. That was progress. *Where is Sophie going?*

Sophie walked back to her car with a box from the bakery. Nothing shook off a bad mood like fresh pastry. She pulled out of the Main Street parking spot and headed for the supermarket. She loved being in town. She didn't know anyone yet, but just being in Cedar Creek made her feel like she belonged to something simple and good. Unlike home. She remembered feeling like that about the city. She used to feel an electrical energy in the city that seemed to propel people through their days and through life. There was nothing a person couldn't find in the city. And when the energy overwhelmed her, she would hole up in her tiny apartment and recharge. How she used to love her life there—until everything changed.

Stopping herself before she went any further, Sophie looked at the blue sky and rewrapped her scarf around her neck. *Why dwell on bad memories?* It was winter, and Christmas was coming. She sailed through the grocery store, picking up the ingredients for a week's worth of comfort food. That, a glass of wine, and Christmas movies and books would fill her days to overflowing. Life was good.

Once home, she made split pea soup in her electric pressure cooker. When it was cool enough, she poured it into a couple of her grandmother's old canning jars. She looked out the window and made sure Cole was home. Then she threw on her coat and headed over to his cabin. She knocked, and he opened the door.

In the midst of her little dance accident, she'd missed some details, like how broad his shoulders were despite his tall, lean frame. And she hadn't seen this expression before. He looked surprised but not necessarily pleasantly.

"I brought you some soup." She held the jar out to him. Sensing his confusion, she felt the need to explain. "I just wanted to thank you for this morning —for helping me after I fell."

"You did thank me."

"I know, but... the thing with soup is it's always too much for one person, so I thought..."

Reluctantly, he said, "Thanks."

"You're welcome." *Oh. This is not going as well as I'd expected.* "Anyway... bye." She grinned and waved before turning and walking away as briskly as one could through six inches of snow. She heard the door close gently behind her. When she got back inside, where it was warm and inviting, she put her jacket on a hook and went into the kitchen.

What was that? I have no idea, but I know what this is. "Wine time!" She grumbled, "It's not like I kicked his puppy or anything. I just brought him some soup." There was nothing wrong with being neighborly. She shook off her uncomfortable feeling, threw another log on the fire, and snuggled up with a book. A few chapters, a big mug of soup, and her life would be back to the way it should be.

Something magical happened. It snowed. No matter how many seasons she saw come and go, Sophie always found December snow otherworldly. Outside, the big fluffy flakes floating down unhurriedly made the inside, lit in soft amber tones, feel warm and cozy.

She fell asleep in her chair by the fire.

5

The next morning, the white landscape looked pristine. Rich-green cedar trees punctured the blanket of snow while the creek seemed to have sunken into its frozen banks. No feet had trod anywhere within sight. The sun had been up long enough to melt the surface to an icy sheen. A slight warming trend was in the forecast, which meant this was the perfect time to clear the driveway before the snow became wet and heavy.

Sophie had lived in the city so long, she couldn't remember the last time she'd cleared a driveway, but she remembered her father going out to start up the snowblower. She squinted as she tried to recall her father's instructions. It was all a bit hazy. *But how hard could it be to turn on a snowblower?* She would remember once she got started. *Just like riding a bicycle.*

She found the model number on the machine in the garage and downloaded the manual to her phone from the manufacturer's website. Step-by-step, she followed the instructions, but nothing happened. No problem. She would reread them and figure it out. She methodically went through the procedure again. And again.

An hour later, Sophie picked up a shovel and started to heave shovels of snow. There was nothing to it the first few times. But as she surveyed the driveway, she realized it was long when measured by snow-loaded shovels. She evaluated her progress. Not inclined to take a deep dive into the math, she settled on something akin to a drop in the bucket. She calculated that her time of completion would be sometime next Tuesday. Refusing to accept defeat, she continued to shovel for another hour. Then, exhausted and thoroughly frustrated, she heaved the shovel. With immediate regret, because she would have to retrieve it, she eyed the shovel halfway across the snow-covered yard. Deciding that was as good a place for it as any, she stormed inside, gulped lukewarm coffee, then returned to the harsh elements to face her dastardly foe.

First, there was the matter of the shovel. She

heaved a deep sigh then tromped through the snow to retrieve it. By the time she returned to the driveway, she was sure she needed a nap. Pushing through her fatigue, she resumed her repetitive and unrewarding task while making a mental note to park close to the road before the next snowfall.

Thirty minutes into the latest phase of Sophie's torment, Cole emerged from his lair, looking hardy and enthused by the bracing air. *Great, just what I need—an audience.* To her surprise, he ducked into a shed and returned with a shovel over his shoulder. *Show-off!*

But instead of starting work on his driveway, he came over to hers. "Looks like you could use some help."

Am I so obviously pathetic? Don't answer that. Yes. Trying to sound as though she were taking it in stride, she said, "Yeah. My grandmother's snow-blower is broken."

"Your grandmother's?"

"Yeah, this is her place. I'm just here to... house-sit." She couldn't believe she'd almost told him she'd lost her job and moved out of her apartment because she couldn't pay the rent. Financial advisors always recommended having months of savings for such an event. Financial advisors could tell that to her paycheck. She had nothing against financial management, but by the time she'd paid rent and utilities, she was lucky to have subway fare to get to and from work. Ah, well, at least that problem was solved. She wasn't going anywhere now.

"Mind if I take a look at it?"

She'd been so lost in thought that it took her a moment to realize what he was talking about. "The snowblower? Sure."

He went into the garage. The first thing he did was to check the fuel.

"Oh, come on! Do you really think I wouldn't check that?"

He looked up with twinkling eyes. "Nothing personal." He fiddled with some levers and knobs, then he changed the plug to a different outlet and tried to start it again. "Starter's broken."

Sophie nodded. "Ah... That explains why it wouldn't start."

He avoided her gaze but appeared to be suppressing a smile. He adjusted a couple more knobs, prompting Sophie to wonder whether that was just something guys did to kill time. It looked more productive—and maybe impressive—than standing and scratching one's head. Although his head was impressive enough. His thick, caramel-colored hair had just enough wave to look good tousled or combed. It seemed always to land in the right place to frame his rugged face. That was a gift Sophie would give anything for. With no warning, her wiry sable hair could spring into action like a scared cartoon cat. "Thick and unruly" was how her mother had described it when she was a child. Even now, she knew that removing her hat was out of the question. Like a wild-eyed thoroughbred horse, her hair would need a good rubdown after this workout before it would be calm enough to be seen out in public.

Speaking of public, she would never be in it again if she didn't clear this driveway. "Well, that's that. I guess I'll just go make some calls to find someone to plow it."

"Why? I'll just start it the old-fashioned way."

"And what's that? Rub two sticks together and blow?"

He laughed. She had not expected that. *Well, go figure.*

Cole proceeded to yank on what looked like a lawnmower cord. Then a miracle happened! It started! It was all she could do not to hug him. She felt like they'd struck oil, and it was spewing all over the place, to her unmatched delight. Actually, that was snow. It was snowing again.

Sophie refocused. At that point, while Cole cut through row after row of snow, Sophie noticed what a strapping specimen he was. He steered that beast with the power of his broad shoulders and sturdy arms. She reflected on that as he rounded a corner. Even in a knit cap, which no one looked good in, no one could deny he was attractive. Although why that was relevant to his snow-blowing skill, she couldn't have said. They were just idle thoughts that came to her, like making note of a beautiful day or admiring pine branches weighted down with snow. Cole was a masculine guy who knew his way around power equipment. There was nothing wrong with noticing that.

That was where it ended, though. She could look but not touch. She had come here to recover from the blow her self-esteem and bank account had suffered for reasons beyond her control. Her grandmother had insisted. "It's good to care for other people, but now it's time for you to take care of yourself."

Grandma Kate got her. The hopelessness of her plight had been wearing her down. Now she had a wonderful opportunity to take a time-out from life and reset. But nothing had the power to stress a girl out more than a guy, so Cole was off-limits.

Besides, he wasn't even her type. She liked guys who were nice. Cole was, to put it kindly, aloof. When he did lower himself to converse with her, he looked pained. And that bothered her. She was not such a horrible person. Some guys had even found her attractive and pleasant to be with. But not this guy. Anytime he was forced to look in her direction, he wound up looking through her. So, no matter how ruggedly handsome he might be, there was no magic happening there. Which was great because she did not want that! Everything was proceeding according to plan.

To be fair, in contrast to his usual manner, Cole had done some nice things. He had run to her aid when she fell. That was nice—embarrassing, but nice. He would have called an ambulance if she'd needed one. That alone deserved a high spot on her list of dating criteria. So from now on, she would absolutely not date a guy who would not call an ambulance if she were critically injured. So there! Cole had ticked one box on her list, which reminded her—there was no actual list. But now that she had some time, she would make one. This retreat was all about self-improvement, so that had to count. *One step forward. Good for me.*

When he finished the driveway, Cole moved on to his. He did give her the courtesy of asking to borrow her snowblower first. As it happened, he didn't have one, which rebalanced his actions on her scale. Had he fixed her snowblower to be nice, or did he just need to clear out his driveway? *Hard to say.* She decided to give him the benefit of the doubt.

Trusting her neighbor was an important component to her peace of mind. In a world full of bears, it didn't hurt to have friends. But mainly, this was her happy place. Anything that interfered with that wasn't allowed.

Cole brought the snowblower back and returned it to its place in the garage. "Thanks for the loaner."

Sophie shrugged. "No problem. I'll make you a deal. If you'll start the snowblower, you can use it all season."

With a grin, he said, "I'll take you up on that."

"Good." She hesitated then said, "Have you eaten? I've got some bagels from the village. If you haven't been there, I highly recommend Cedar Creek Bagels. They're amazing."

He smiled, not the kind that lit his eyes, but a polite smile with excuses behind it. "Thanks, but I've got some stuff to do."

Ah, stuff. You can't put that off. "Okay. See you next time it snows." She laughed to herself and went inside. All that talk of bagels had made her hungry.

Cole went inside and scrounged for some food. He hadn't done as good a job of shopping as he'd thought. He'd forgotten he wasn't a short walk or phone call away from quick takeout or delivery, so he'd come home with his usual staples. But a man couldn't live on peanut butter and jelly alone. He opened the fridge and spied Sophie's soup. He couldn't remember the last time he'd had split pea soup. It wasn't something he ever ordered in a restaurant, which meant he probably hadn't eaten it since he was a child.

Do I even like split pea soup? It didn't sound like the sort of thing people went around raving about, like pizza or a huge plate of nachos. He opened it and gave it a sniff. *Hmm. Not bad, actually.* She'd left a note on masking tape she'd stuck to the jar. "If a spoon stands up in it—and it probably will—just add water until it looks like soup again."

Following her directions, he combined the soup with a little water and heated the soup in a pot on the camp stove. Minutes later, the hot soup smelled pretty good. He poured it into a bowl then slurped a spoonful.

Oh wow! I might need to rethink this thing with the neighbor. If this soup was any indication, that breakfast he'd just turned down was a missed opportunity. He dug in and ate more, then he tipped the bowl up and drank it. Repeating the previous steps, he added water and warmed the rest of the soup. He proceeded to down it in what would be record time if there were a pea-soup-eating record. Then he pondered the protocol for neighborly sharing. A vague childhood memory came to mind of people returning casserole dishes to his mother when she'd taken them food. Why had she done that? That was anyone's guess. All he knew was that he wanted more of that soup. If he hadn't turned down her invitation, he would be over there eating more now.

People made mistakes that came back through the years to haunt them with nagging regret. Turning down that bagel was one of those mistakes. Cole set about devising a plan for more soup.

6

Winter fishing wasn't for everyone. Even those who habitually engaged in the sport tended to land on a continuum. There were those who erected shanties on the frozen lakes for the season yet still needed sleds to haul out essentials, otherwise known as beer. But Cole preferred fly fishing in the rivers and streams. While lakes might have been peppered with ice fishermen, Cole preferred to be completely alone. Something about the solitude of fly fishing cleared his head and put things into perspective. He needed perspective right now.

His phone rang, breaching his first rule of ice fishing. He'd forgotten to turn the thing off. He'd only brought it for safety, although what good it would do him, he couldn't have articulated. Getting a signal was iffy, at best. Besides, if the ice cracked and he fell through, was he really going to make a quick phone call for help? Probably not.

"Hello?"

"Cole!"

"Dad? Hi."

Quietly, his father said, "I didn't want to intrude. I know you went there to be alone."

Cole glanced about. He couldn't have been more alone.

"But your mother was worried."

She would be. Cole smiled. He had his father's temperament, so his father understood Cole's need to retreat now and then. But no matter how he'd tried to reassure his mother about this latest detour in life, she worried.

Cole said, "I don't mind."

"So, how are you?" He could hear the smile in his father's voice. "Be thorough. I'll need to give a full accounting."

"I'm good. It's like a vacation." A vacation that came with no job to return to and a subtle yet nagging sensation that life had tossed him aside like the spinet from a pioneer's westward-bound wagon. "I'm ice fishing right now."

"Fantastic! I wish I were there."

Emotion welled up from deep within him and caught Cole by surprise. "Me too."

His father cleared his throat. "So, how's the cabin? I can't remember the last time someone stayed there."

"It needs some work, but I'm up for a project."

"There's no reason for you to bear the brunt of all that. I'll send you a check in the morning."

"You don't have to do that. Oh! I've got something on the line. Give my love to Mom!"

"I will. Take care, Cole."

"I will. Bye, Dad."

Cole looked at the phone for a moment, put it back in his pocket, then swallowed back his emotions. He focused on the fish on his line, longing for the trust and contentment he'd felt as a child fishing with his father. Back then, life was good, and the future was his to take hold of. Where had the world lost its way?

The world would have to take care of itself while he reeled in this fish. *Here comes dinner.*

On the way home, Cole stopped for potatoes, vegetables, beer, and a few other food items. Then he made one more stop for a bottle of wine. It would be a simple meal, but he would put freshly grilled trout up there with his neighborhood restaurants in the city. It felt good to look forward to something. As he thought through how he would season and grill it, he realized he had too much fish for one person, and he didn't have a freezer. He could have thrown one of the fish back, but it was too late now. When he went into town next, he would pick up an ice chest.

In the meantime, he wondered if Sophie liked fish. His cooking didn't come close to hers, but he knew how to grill a fresh trout. He owed her, according to the neighborly rules his mother lived by. To share his dinner with her—as a neighbor and friend—was a perfectly good thing to do.

He pulled into his driveway, left the groceries and fish on the counter, went back outside, and headed toward Sophie's cottage. As he knocked on the door, he began to have doubts. He didn't want to give her the wrong impression. He wasn't looking for a relationship, just someone to share fish with. She hadn't answered the door. She might not even be home. He turned to leave.

The door opened. "Cole." She looked surprised.

Of course. Why wouldn't she? "How do you feel about fish?"

"As pets or for dinner?" Her eyebrows furrowed as she smiled.

"Oh." That hadn't come across at all how he'd

intended. What if she was a vegetarian? He'd probably offended her.

Sophie took mercy. "I was kidding! I love fish. Why do you ask?"

"I caught a couple of trout. It's too much for one person. Would you like some?"

"Only if I don't have to clean it or cook it." She winced. "I'm sorry. That sounded really demanding. I just don't know how to cook fish."

Relieved, Cole said, "Well, I do. I was going to grill it. I can bring yours over when I'm finished."

Since knocking on the door, he had seen several versions of confusion on her face, but this was a new one. "Oh, we could do that. Or, while you're grilling, I could cook some rice and vegetables to go with it."

"I've got some."

"Great! Why don't you bring them over, and I'll get started?"

"Okay. Be right back." Cole suddenly felt as though his little gesture had spun out of control. This was sounding like dinner together—or even a date—which was not what he'd ever intended. He was just sharing fish. Now she was cooking side dishes to go with it, which implied they would be eating together. Cole did the math. Two people eating together equaled a date. He couldn't have explained why that seemed like such a monumental event. He just wasn't

himself. His life was out of focus. He barely wanted
to eat. He sure as hell didn't want to date. He had
nothing to offer—but fish. So now he and Sophie were
having dinner.

He returned five minutes later with the vegetables and a bottle of wine. If that didn't look like a
date, nothing did. Poor Sophie. She was about to be
disappointed. She took the vegetables and wine.

With a nod toward his cabin, Cole said, "I'll go
get the fire started."

"I've got an outdoor fireplace here in the back.
Wouldn't it be easier to use that so you could keep a
closer eye on it?"

*That would mean I'd be here, and we'd have to
talk.* He didn't know what to say. If only he'd stayed
home, grilled his fish, and kept his life simple, but this
wasn't Sophie's fault. So he said, "Okay."

Cole kept busy grilling, drank some beer, turned
the fish, and drank some more beer. Then it was
finished. He came inside and sat down at her table.
There was a fire in the fireplace, and the place was
aglow in soft light, with a warm, cozy feeling that his
cabin lacked. In short, he felt good. That was the beer
talking—or thinking.

Sophie looked up from her plate, fork in hand.
"So you left city life to vacation in your family's
cabin?"

It felt like a question, so he explained. "It's not a vacation. I've moved here."

"I don't blame you. It's so nice here, isn't it?"

He began to concoct an explanation of why he'd moved here, when she surprised him by not following up with more questions. That was what people did. They asked questions. They followed up with more questions. He could blame courtroom dramas, but he couldn't blame Sophie. She was just making conversation. He said, "Yes, it's better than nice."

"That's how I feel." She smiled and looked down.

She was shy. He hadn't noticed at first, but beneath her easy manner, he detected shyness. That was something he could understand—not that he had ever been bashful. He'd always been confident and even competitive in certain situations, like bicycle races. But he'd lost that competitive spirit when his business and life went up in flames. He hadn't expected what he said next, but the words just came out of his mouth. "I needed to get away."

She held his gaze. "I get that."

He wanted to fire back, *You couldn't possibly get that*. But something in her eyes told him she did. She might not know what he had gone through, but he saw the same look in her eyes that he sometimes saw in the mirror.

She continued. "My grandmother offered her cottage because the world failed to meet my expectations." She laughed, seemingly aware of how absurd she must sound, but Cole nodded.

He understood. They had something in common. Without knowing each other's details, they shared a connection.

Her eyes brightened. "This fish was amazing!" And with that, she'd brought them back from a place they both seemed to know well and didn't want to be in. Knowing they shared something neither cared to discuss established a baseline for their relationship. Although Cole barely knew Sophie, being with her reminded him of what it used to feel like to be happy.

Together, they washed dishes and talked about favorite Christmas memories. Cole hadn't laughed in so long. It felt good. Somehow, she talked him into playing cards. Of course, she had a special Christmas deck with Santa and his reindeer, but Cole didn't even mind. A week ago, he would have scoffed at anyone who suggested he would be sitting by the fire, playing cards with a pretty girl. She was pretty. That wouldn't have been the first thing he would have said about her if he had to describe her to someone else. There were other, more noticeable aspects, like her singing and dancing, along with her dogged desire to spread Christmas cheer. It wasn't forced. That was just how she was. She lightened the air in a room.

After they finished another game, they both scooped up the cards, and their fingers touched. Like a spark from a fire, it was gone as soon as it happened.

Cole stood. "Thanks."

"For eating your fish?" Her eyes twinkled. "You're welcome. Anytime." He hadn't flinched or done anything he would have thought visible, but she reacted. It was slight, just a fleeting widening of the eyes.

He suddenly felt the need to define things between them. The energy arcing between them was palpable. She had to feel it. But that sort of feeling led to relationships. A few years ago, when life was good and he was happy, he would have welcomed the excitement of new possibilities. From this evening alone, he knew they would have fun together, but the timing was bad. He couldn't drag someone into his life until he was whole. Of course, there was no way of explaining all that without sounding like a presumptuous ass. She might be thinking, "This guy is a mess. Run away!"

So he said, "See you next time it snows. Oh—and if you find yourself with soup you need to get rid of, I'm your man."

"So you liked it?"

"Loved it!"

She looked pleased. "Pea soup isn't for everyone, so I'm glad you liked it."

"I did."

"If you bring back the jar, I'll refill it next time I make soup."

"Oh, crap. I knew I forgot something."

She laughed. "Relax. I'm sure you're good for it." Her smile was warm.

Cole felt a sudden impulse to kiss her. There was a moment when time seemed to pause, waiting just for that kiss. It didn't happen.

She said, "Be careful walking home. It's dark out there."

He nodded. "My first night here, I left a flashlight on all night. I probably shouldn't admit that. I've just destroyed your impression of me as a manly outdoorsman, haven't I?"

"Yeah, pretty much. Oh, I've got an idea. I might have some rope around here. You could hang onto one end, and if you get lost, I could pull you back here to start over."

Cole laughed. "That sounds a little sad—especially since I could see myself doing it."

She gazed into his eyes. "I have a feeling you'll find your way just fine."

To my cabin, maybe. I'm not so sure about life. But

as he stood there with Sophie, her peaceful and unhurried manner drew him into a like frame of mind. He suddenly wished he didn't have to leave. He turned and, with a wave, headed for home.

Cole, you can like her as a friend and a neighbor, but don't complicate life by wanting more.

7

Sophie poured a glass of wine and sat down by the fire. Idly, she picked up a book then set it down on her lap unopened, preferring to gaze at the fire and indulge in her thoughts. Portions of the evening replayed in her head. She didn't like to admit it, but she couldn't deny that she found Cole intriguing. They shared an unspoken sense of kinship. They were two lost souls caught up in a journey they didn't want to be on. Whatever it was, neither had wanted to share it. For that, she was grateful. Her pit of despair was a one-seater. Still, she couldn't ignore the elusive connection they shared. It made her curious when what she needed was to stop reflecting on his every word and deed. And she needed to stop finding him so darned attractive.

On the plus side, the fact that she found him

attractive disproved her family's assumption that she was running away from the world to wallow in self-pity. They had it all wrong. What Sophie wanted was to hide out in an insulated world where people were kind and looked out for each other. The only way to ensure such a world was to be alone. Here, she could create the life that she wanted, and right now, what she wanted was Christmas. It was a time of new birth and hope. Joy might be too much to ask at the moment, but peace would be more than enough.

She made up her mind to make a list of all the Christmas events in the village nearby. She was going to attend those that interested her, but first, she was going to make cookies.

She looked up. *That's it!* She was going to cook, but not just cookies—a meal. She would cook Christmas dinner! Years ago, the whole family used to come to the cottage for Christmas. Then Grandma Kate moved to Florida, and they stopped. *But this year, it would be magical if they all came here for Christmas.*

She got up and started looking through recipe books, many of which were still there. But one was missing—the one she needed most. That book was the oldest, with scraps of handwritten recipes sticking out of the ends. Tomorrow, she would call her grandmother and ask if she had them. If she could get Matt to leave his gaming chair, he could take phone pics of the recipes and text them to her. He might take some convincing, but food was a powerful motivator. In the meantime, she would make a list of her favorites.

Morning sun washed the windows in light as Sophie made phone calls and holiday plans. To her delight, everyone in the family was on board with having Christmas at the cottage. She was in holiday bliss. The cottage was already charming enough, but the Christmas decorating she'd done made it perfect. It just needed a tree.

She put on her favorite holiday carol playlist and smiled, wholly content. Cedar branches covered the beams in the kitchen, and embers glowed red in the wood-burning stove. Scattered baking ingredients covered the counter, while flour and sugar dusted the surface. But the best part of all was the aroma of gingerbread filling the air. Sophie paused, coffee in hand, and drew in a deep breath. *This is Christmas.*

She had just pulled the last of the cookies from the oven when a knock at the door startled her. She wiped her hands on a towel and answered the door. "Hi, Cole."

"Oh my gosh, what is that? Gingerbread?"

Sophie nodded. "Cookies, not bread—although I should make some of that too." She nodded cheerily. "Gingerbread with freshly whipped cream on top." If the scent of her cookies could reduce a grown man—a grown and very masculine man—to his inner child, then her morning's efforts had been worth it.

He lifted an eyebrow. "Well, that changes everything."

"What changes what?"

He shook his head with regret. "I hate to do this to you, but I'm going to have to raise my price for starting your snowblower this season."

She had no idea what he was talking about, so she waited for him to explain.

"The deal now includes cookies. To be fair, I won't make unreasonable demands."

She smiled, giving in to his charms. "That's good to know."

He pretended to be very serious. "Any flavor will do—gingerbread, sugar, chocolate chip. I'm not picky."

Sophie played along, looking reluctant. "You drive a hard bargain, but okay, come here."

Handing him a napkin, she pointed to a cooling rack of cookies. "Help yourself."

Cole narrowed his eyes. "Is this some kind of a trick? Am I about to burn my tongue?"

"I can't say that that didn't occur to me, but the batch on that rack was the first to come out. You'll be fine. They might be a little warm. You'll probably need some milk to go with them."

He fixed his eyes on hers. "I forgot about milk. Milk has to be part of the deal too."

Sophie sucked air in through her teeth and shook her head slowly. "Oh, I don't know about that. That might be a dealbreaker."

He looked up with a sigh. "Okay, I'll throw in some fish."

Sophie wrinkled her brow. "There's only so much fish a person can eat in one holiday season."

Then he blurted out, "Fine, then I'll take you to lunch." Things were suddenly not quite so funny. A series of expressions crossed over Cole's face. Then, as if he hadn't suggested it in the first place, he said, "Why not? Have you eaten?"

"What time is it?" Sophie had woken up early. She wasn't a morning person, but sometimes her insomnia struck at the other end of her sleep cycle. So she had risen early, had some coffee, and set about baking.

He glanced at his watch then looked disappointed. "Ten o'clock. It sure felt like lunchtime."

One of the things that had made Sophie so good at her 911 job was her skill at problem-solving.

Forgetting that they hadn't been negotiating an actual deal, she faced the problem head-on and solved it. "We can have brunch." Then she wondered what had just happened. She didn't mind throwing a couple of cookies his way, but she wasn't quite sure how she had gotten caught up in planning to go out together. It didn't matter how casual it sounded. This was a meal with a male, which sounded a lot like a date.

His expression changed as he watched her reaction, prompting her to realize that her face must have telegraphed every thought she'd just had—either that or he could read minds. "I mean, it's just lunch—I mean, brunch—between friends."

That doesn't sound quite so bad. Friends... eating brunch. It's not even a meal, technically. "Oh, of course. And we both have to eat." She shrugged and almost convinced herself of what she was saying. But for two people who were no more than friends, they both looked enthused by the prospect.

Cole said, "Good. Let's go."

Sophie's hands shot to her hair, where stubborn strands seemed about to take flight in any direction. "I need a few minutes, well, twenty, to get ready." She looked at the clock. "Let's meet at..."

"Now? Okay, sounds perfect!"

She shook her head, but before she could speak,

he said, "This is going to sound just insane, but let's be two crazy kids and just go out as we are?"

A couple of things about that statement bothered Sophie. It implied that she played things too safe and was too buttoned up. She wasn't like that at all. She could be spontaneous. But when she tried to think of a recent example of her spontaneity, she came up empty. It stunned her to realize that he could be right. They'd barely met, yet he thought he had her all figured out, and that wouldn't do. So she proved him wrong. "Fine. Let's just go. This is me being unpredictable."

"I knew you'd say that."

She opened her mouth to protest, but he laughed. "I'm just messing with you. Come on. Let's go."

Sophie wanted to be annoyed, but when he laughed, he had a dimple that looked good—good enough to distract her. Before she had time to think it through, she grabbed her purse and followed him out the door.

8

The village of Cedar Creek went all out for Christmas. Cole had nothing against Christmas decorations. He even appreciated the festive air they lent to the holiday season—in moderation. Yet as he stood on the main street that ran through the village, he found himself thoroughly enjoying the evergreens and colored Christmas lights. All the storefronts were decked out so that Main Street resembled a Dickensian village. The weather had cooperated by coating the world in a fresh layer of snow. In the center of town was a square with a small gazebo containing a Christmas tree. Looking as charming and quaint as it did, the gazebo almost seemed to have been conjured by some sort of Christmas enchantment in the mist from an era gone by. No one could take in the sight and not feel an inkling of holiday spirit.

It didn't take long to choose where they would eat. A block from the square was a chrome railroad car diner. Both having lived in the city, Cole and Sophie each held a deep-seated appreciation for diner food. Unable to choose between breakfast or lunch, they ordered an omelet and patty melt, then ate half of each to the accompaniment of top-forty Christmas tunes from the tabletop jukebox.

Halfway through the meal, Cole realized he'd lost the defeated mood that had been weighing him down.

As if reading his mind, Sophie said, "Coming here was the right thing to do."

"To the diner?" Cole's mouth quirked at the corner.

"That too. But the mountains are good for the soul."

"I agree." Until now, Cole hadn't wanted to pry, but in a way, Sophie had opened the door. "So what brought you here?"

When she hesitated to answer, Cole regretted having asked.

"I lost my job."

"Which was?"

She told him and described her last few days at work. "With no job, I couldn't keep my apartment, so moving was more of a necessity than a choice. I was fully prepared to move into my parents' basement when my grandmother offered her cottage. She must have picked up on my stress level and taken pity on me. Anyway, she told me to stay here and take some time to regroup. And that's what I'm doing. It's surprising how a change like this can make things look clearer. Wow. Listen to me rambling on. Are you sorry you asked?"

"No, not at all! And I know what you mean about seeing things clearer. Life is different in a small town like this. People work hard, but they take time to help one another—even strangers like me. Most of all, people listen. It's becoming a lost art."

Sophie nodded. "That's what makes life interesting—hearing what others think."

Cole looked about at the busy waiters and at the customers chatting and enjoying their meals. "I know. The evening I got out of the hospital—"

Sophie set her fork down. "Hold on! Hospital?"

Cole forgot he hadn't told her that part of his story. After he filled her in up to the hospital stay, he said, "After my parents picked me up, I was desperate for a good meal, so we went to my favorite neighborhood cafe. I had to have one of their burgers. We had just begun eating when a large group—they looked like students from the university—turned a corner and headed down the street. I didn't think much of it until they turned over a table and yelled in some diners' faces. We ducked onto a side street and returned to my apartment."

Sophie's sympathetic gaze made him slightly uneasy. He hadn't meant to elicit that sort of response. He was just stating facts.

"That must've been hard for your parents."

"I think it shook them up, but we recovered over peanut butter and jelly sandwiches." He smiled at the memory. "My mom is like that. No matter what happens, she always rallies and gives the appearance of calm."

"And your father?"

"He's the philosophical one. He couldn't figure out what they'd hoped to gain. But then, that's never been his style. He never got angry when I was a child, or at least he didn't show it. He would leave me alone for a while to reflect on whatever it was, then he would ask me questions—the sort of questions that made me realize that my choices were crap." He laughed. "Sometimes the guilt just about did me in. But the thing was, he listened to me, and I learned to listen to him. I didn't want to disappoint him."

Emotions nearly overwhelmed him as he thought of his parents. He was noticing signs of age, slight but undeniable reminders of the fleeting nature of life—of their lives.

Cole exhaled. "Anyway, after he got over his 'What the hell was that?' moment, he was more curious than anything else. He couldn't figure out why they would force people to hear and yet make it impossible for them to listen."

Sophie said, "I think I'd like your parents."

"I think they'd like you."

Their eyes locked. In the midst of lively holiday music and conversational blur, between Cole and Sophie, the world became still. They both looked away, but the silence lingered.

The waiter came by with their check. Cole insisted on paying, so Sophie left the tip, and they left. After passing the gazebo, they veered off the road and crossed a path that led through the park to a pond. In winter, it became the village ice skating rink. Cole and Sophie stood and watched for a minute or so.

Then Sophie looked at Cole with twinkling eyes. "Come on."

"Come on what?" He knew the answer, but he hesitated.

Sophie tugged on his elbow. "You know what. Let's go rent some skates."

She was glowing, but he wasn't sure he was ready for skating. During the looting, his legs had escaped injury, but if he fell, which was likely, his arms might not fare too well. But as he looked at her face, keen with anticipation, he couldn't tell her no. So he shrugged, and minutes later, they were on the ice, skating together.

He hadn't skated since he was a boy. From the looks of it, Sophie wasn't much better. But together, they made their way around the pond several times. Cole nearly fell once but rallied until he felt almost sure-footed. He even managed to keep Sophie from falling at one point. In that instant, as he held her in his arms, he thought he might stop breathing. After she recovered her balance, she took hold of his hand, and they continued to skate hand in hand. When they finally stopped, she slipped her hand free, leaving his feeling empty.

They got two hot chocolates and sat in an outdoor cafe overlooking the pond. Cole felt more than mere Christmas spirit, but he held it in check. This was no time to be starting a relationship. Indulging in his feelings for Sophie would complicate life. He was in a sort of limbo, with no idea where his life might be heading. A relationship wouldn't be fair to either of them. Although his life seemed to be settling down in Cedar Creek, Sophie was more or less on an extended vacation. Sooner or later, she would leave. There was no point in investing in something—in someone—when neither of them could follow through. Of course, that assumed she had any feelings for him. He was way over his skis on that count.

With a deep breath, Cole forced himself to look beyond his enchanting surroundings and remember reality, a place where he lived.

Sophie turned and said, "Thank you."

At first, Cole thought he might have missed something she'd just said. He'd been deep in thought.

She laughed at his confusion. "Sorry. I have a really bad habit of thinking then continuing my thoughts out loud. What I meant was, thank you for this. It has felt so good to be out doing Christmassy things. I've been in kind of a funk, but you've brought me out of it. So thank you."

"I can't take credit. In fact, I should thank you. I've been through a rough patch. But today almost felt normal."

Sophie drew in an excited breath. "We should do all the Christmas things!"

Cole wasn't ready for that. "All? Just how many are there?"

"As many as we can fit into the days before Christmas." Her delight deflated. "You're frowning."

"No, I'm just thinking."

"Oh." She looked down at her hands. "Sorry, I got carried away."

"That's okay." He meant it. He loved her enthusiasm. He just wasn't sure he wanted to be enthusiastic with her. She set the bar pretty high.

To his surprise, her eyes filled with tears. "Can we leave?"

"Sure." By the time they got back to his truck, Cole was certain he'd said something wrong. He just wasn't sure what. Once seated with the truck idling and the warmth of the heater working, Cole said, "I'm sorry."

She turned, eyes now dry. "Why? You didn't do anything wrong. This is probably going to sound weird, but all the recent events in my life caught up with me back there. I've been soldiering on as though nothing were wrong, but then—I don't know. My feelings exploded all over the place. I'm so sorry."

"That's okay." He would have been lying if he said it hadn't thrown him off-balance, but he didn't mind. "You're human. Feelings happen."

"No, really, this isn't like me. I'm usually so calm and logical. I can handle a 911 emergency, get help to people, then talk them calmly through it. I don't know what happened."

He smiled gently. "Maybe life happened."

She looked into his eyes. "Yeah, it did."

He pivoted on the seat to face her directly and took her hand in both of his. He did it without thinking, but there they were—her hands in his. Then he surprised himself by saying, "I would love to do Christmas things with you."

She cast a knowing look at him. "You don't have to say that."

"I know, but I'm saying it." There was so much he wanted to add to that statement. It didn't matter what sorts of things, Christmas or not—he just wanted to do them with her because that would make her happy.

And that was a problem. She might not have any feelings for him, but it was too late to deny what he felt. All he could do now was try to guard his heart.

9

Sophie was happy. That was something she hadn't felt in weeks, and she liked it. She liked Cole. As he pulled into the driveway, she stole another look at his profile, from his alert eyes to his high cheekbones, well-formed jaw, and full lips. She couldn't deny being attracted to him, but she would deny the deeper feelings that threatened to spring to life in her heart. As soon as she could find a job, she'd be leaving, while he didn't look like he was going anyplace soon. Their lives were on pause for the moment, but when they moved on, it would be in different directions. The more she let herself feel now, the more pain she would have later.

Sophie was a problem solver. That was one thing she knew she did well. In this case, the solution was easy enough: Be friends. Have fun and enjoy the holidays, but do so as friends. Later on, when it was time to leave, they would be able to part and move on with minimal pain. Problem solved.

It was too bad it had to be that way. She liked Cole already, but being with him around other people gave her a more objective perspective. He always had a few pleasant words to say to the waiter and the woman who sold the hot chocolate. Sophie watched their eyes light up in response to Cole's easy conversation and genuine interest. He put people at ease. She liked that about him.

Cole pulled his key from the ignition. "So, what Christmas event is on the agenda for tomorrow?"

"I don't know. What do you love about Christmas? Name one thing."

He stared at the woods behind the cabin. "When I was a kid, it was all about presents."

Sophie shook her head. "Not good enough."

Cole narrowed his eyes. "It's Christmas! Presents have to count!"

"Well, okay. But it's too early for that. Name something else."

"Christmas tree lights?"

Sophie gasped with delight. "Oh, that's it! That was easy."

He furrowed his eyebrows. "It was?"

"Yes. What step comes before Christmas tree lights?"

"Untangling them?"

She rolled her eyes. "Where do you hang them?"

With a glint in his eyes, he said, "In the house?"

"On the...?"

"First day of Christmas?" He laughed.

Sophie narrowed her eyes. "Very funny. The tree! We need a tree!"

"Good point." For someone who thought it was such a good point, he didn't look very convinced. "Don't you think it's a bit early for a tree?"

That was just crazy talk. "What month is it?"

His face wrinkled up as though she were the one talking crazy. "December."

Sophie lifted her palms. "There you have it."

"Okay...?"

He seemed to need things spelled out for him. "So tomorrow, we'll go to a Christmas tree farm."

"Oh, okay." For some reason Sophie couldn't pinpoint, he didn't seem on board with the plan.

Her eyebrows drew together. "You made a face."

"No, I did not make a face."

"Yes, you did. What were you thinking?"

"Uh... visions of cranky kids danced in my head."

Sophie was not amused. "You don't have to go. I'm fine. I get it. But I need a tree, so I'm going." She lifted her eyebrows and smiled, hoping she looked neutral enough. They were clearly not on the same page, but that wasn't his fault. She began to have doubts about the whole Christmas activity thing.

"Sophie, one thing you should know about me is that I can't lie. I've got the worst poker face in the world, so if I didn't want to go, you would know it."

She hesitated but chose to be honest. "Well, you kind of looked like—"

"I wanted to go? That's because I do."

"Are you sure?"

He smiled warmly. "Positive."

"Well, good. Then we'll go to a Christmas tree farm. Then tomorrow night—tree decorating!"

Cole's eyebrows drew together. "That's a whole lot of Christmas for one day."

Sophie peered quizzically at him.

Cole explained, "I think the tree should count as one thing, then decorating it is another."

Sophie studied him, unsure of whether or not he was serious. She decided he was. "Well, okay. We wouldn't want to tire you out." She couldn't help but smile.

"Oh, come on!" Cole looked away and shook his head. "The truth is, I need time at some point to go ice fishing."

"Fair enough."

His eyes lit up. "Which can be our next Christmas activity!" He grinned smugly.

Squinting from confusion, she waited for him to explain.

"Fishing," he said as if it were obvious.

"That's not really a Christmas activity."

"To be fair, if I'm going to let you drag me to a Christmas tree farm—"

"Drag you? You said you wanted to go!"

His eyes twinkled. "I was just being nice."

Sophie wasn't buying it, nor was she buying a fishing expedition. For one thing, she didn't like raw fish, and she refused to touch bait. Then she thought of an out. Triumphantly folding her arms, she said, "Well, Mr. Nice Guy, unless you can explain what's so Christmassy about fishing, I'm not gonna go." She had him. The argument was won.

Cole said, "Jesus was a fisherman."

"Not when he was a baby!" *Aha!* "So save it for Easter. We're not going fishing for Christmas."

Cole laughed. "I was kidding. I wouldn't put you through that. Winter fishing is an acquired taste. Also cold. But I'll make you a deal. I'll bring the fish back, and we'll have it for dinner."

She narrowed her eyes. "You'll do the cooking?"

Cole nodded.

Abundantly satisfied, Sophie extended her hand,

and they shook on it. Cole let go of her hand but held her gaze. For a moment, Sophie forgot to smile or think.

Cole seemed a little lost, too, but he was first to recover. "So, about this Christmas tree farm expedition. Do you know where one is?"

"Funny you should ask. No. I'll do some research."

Cole shrugged. "I'll trust your judgment."

Her eyes sparkled. "As you should."

"So... tree tomorrow, then fishing and dinner. Then the day after that, we can decorate your tree."

A slight frown clouded her face. "You mean our trees—as in two trees—one for each of us."

His expression went blank. "Oh. I hadn't really planned to get a tree myself."

"But you've got to!"

"Why?"

"Because—Christmas!"

Despite a slight hesitation, he gave in. "Okay. I'll do it for you."

"No, do it for yourself. You'll be glad that you did."

With a light laugh, Cole shook his head. "Okay. I guess I'm getting a tree." With a glint in his eye, he said, "Yeah, that might work. It'll give me something to hang my fish on."

Sophie caught herself staring slack-jawed, which made Cole burst out laughing.

"I'm kidding!"

"Of course. I knew that."

They exchanged numbers so they could firm up their plans in the morning, then they parted for the evening with a hug. Cole hadn't meant it to happen. He wasn't even sure who made the first move. But it happened, and he didn't mind.

Later, while Cole sat in front of the fireplace, reflecting on life, he thought a lot about his day—but mainly about Sophie. When he'd arrived at the cabin, he was spent. He hadn't felt anything except relief to be there. Then he met Sophie, and now he felt almost like himself. It wasn't a huge overpowering thing to like Sophie. She made it easy. Together, they just seemed to fit. Simple pleasures like sharing a meal or walking down Main Street were better with Sophie. Being with her was like coming home and being where he belonged.

That thought raised a red flag. He ignored it. He wasn't able to feel happiness yet, but with Sophie, he felt wholly content.

10

Sophie did her homework and located a Christmas tree farm twenty minutes away. It looked perfect. It opened at nine, so at eight fifty-nine, they were at the entrance, all ready to go. At Cole's insistence, their first stop was a shed serving breakfast. They each got breakfast sandwiches on freshly baked bread and tall steaming coffees, then settled on a picnic table near one of the outdoor heaters.

After Cole finished, he leaned back. "That's all I needed. I'm done."

Sophie laughed. "Oh, no, you're not. Let's go find a bow saw."

Once that was accomplished, they were on their way, trudging through rows of trees. The advantage of coming out early was that the farm wasn't yet swarming with people. For acres, all they could see were evergreen trees and white snow.

Sophie grabbed Cole's elbow. "Wait. Listen."

They stood still for a good half minute before Cole whispered, "What?"

"What do you hear?"

"Nothing."

"Exactly. It's perfect." She breathed in the scent of balsam Christmas trees then looked at Cole. "This... is Christmas."

Tiny lines spread from his eyes as he smiled. "I have to admit that you're right."

As she looked into his eyes, it felt almost like sharing a memory.

Sophie snapped out of it. That made no sense. They'd just met. *We're friends. We're getting a tree. That's all.* "Okay, Cole. Time to channel your inner lumberjack. No, wait." She held out her palm and nodded toward the saw. "I've never done this before. I'd like to try."

He turned over the saw and gestured toward the tree. She squatted and started to saw. Several strokes later, she said, "Next year, I'm bringing my own saw. This thing couldn't cut through butter."

"Oh, right. Blame the saw." When she shot a cold look at him, he lifted an eyebrow.

"Fine. You try it."

With a bit of manly arrogance, he crouched beside her and took over. "You just have to... put some... muscle... into it. Crap. I'd be better off with mall food court cutlery."

"Oh, really?" She folded her arms and watched with added pleasure.

In the end, taking turns, they got the job done.

Sophie sat in the snow. She didn't care. "I'm exhausted."

Cole joined her, resting his arms on his knees. "We could have gone with a store-bought tree."

Shocked, Sophie said, "Perish the thought!" She stood and dusted off the snow. "One more to go."

Cole said, "Oh, right. I forgot about that."

"But I didn't. You are so lucky to have me." She hastened to add, "Here. Helping you."

Cole smirked with twinkling eyes. "Lucky me."

"It's just what I do. I'm a helper." She laughed. "Come on. Let's find your tree."

He just couldn't get inspired by trees the way Sophie could. Then he spied a small tree that would fit on his table.

"Are you sure that's not just a branch stuck in the snow?" Sophie studied him for a moment then handed the saw to him. "Okay, Charlie Brown. Have at it."

At Sophie's insistence, they loaded up on lights,

ornaments, and scented candles, then she turned to Cole. "You're welcome."

He gave her the same confused look she'd grown used to, so she explained. "In advance. That's for later, when you're sitting by the fire with your tree and candles. You'll want to thank me, but I won't be there."

He smiled as though he were about to say something but thought better of it.

With two trees in the back of Cole's pickup, they pulled out of the tree farm and headed for home.

Sophie held open the door while Cole carried the Christmas tree into her cottage. "One down, one to go. See? We're halfway there."

Cole set the tree down and exhaled. "I wouldn't exactly call it halfway. My tree is three feet tall and will take maybe ten minutes to decorate. Somehow, I have a feeling yours will take longer."

Sophie poured water into the tree stand. "Well, we do have different decorating styles, but that's half the fun. We can make our trees what we want them to be."

Cole set the tree into its base. "So if that's half the fun, what's the other half?"

Sophie tightened the screws until the tree was secure, then she stood, facing Cole. "Sharing it with someone."

Their eyes met, and he felt an almost irresistible pull toward her. She felt it too. He could see it in her eyes and the way her soft lips parted. He could have kissed her. He wanted to. But what they had together, their friendship, was fragile and fleeting. Crossing over the line with a kiss would be too great a risk. It could break it and tear them apart.

Cole looked away and forced a bright smile. "I have a feeling if I spend enough time with you, I'll be watching sentimental holiday movies and dabbing my eyes with a hanky."

It took her a moment to shift gears, but she faked a smile and said, "I'm not sure I want to see that."

"Me neither. So what's on the agenda after this?"

Sophie wrinkled her brow. "I guess I should scratch my Christmas movie idea."

"See? I knew it! It's all part of your devious plan, isn't it?"

She lifted her hands in surrender. "Busted. I guess if we're scrapping the movie, we'll have to settle for the soup I left in the slow cooker."

"My gosh, is that what that is? It smells amazing."

Her eyes shone in the light. "With any luck, it

will taste just as good. So are you up for some soup and spiked eggnog afterward?"

"Are you kidding me? You can't fill the place with that kind of aroma and expect me to leave."

Looking satisfied, Sophie headed for the kitchen. "If you get a fire going, I'll get the soup."

She paused at the door and turned back, looking mischievous. "Of course, you do realize that without a movie, you'll have to look at me and possibly talk. Aha! See? My plan's more devious than you even suspected!"

He couldn't help it. The mere thought softened his mood, and he unleashed his true feelings. "I wouldn't mind that at all."

She gazed back at him with a gentle look in her eyes. "I wouldn't either."

They stayed up late laughing and talking. They even broke down and watched a Christmas movie. As the credits rolled, Cole joked about the transformation being complete as he lifted his cocktail napkin and pretended to dab his eyes. Even as he did it, he felt another transformation at work in his heart. It was almost too late to turn back. He was falling for her.

Abruptly, Cole stood to leave. "This was a really fun day."

Sophie followed him to the door and waited while he fastened his coat. As he put his scarf around his neck, Sophie reached out and smoothed down the edge. It was a casual gesture until their eyes met, and they froze.

He half whispered, "Sophie."

They closed the space between them and kissed. It was tender, and yet as they pressed close together, Cole felt as though he had stepped too close to the edge. He was the first to pull back, but Sophie wasn't too far behind.

He heard his own husky "I'm sorry," as he tried to read her expression. She looked stunned, but he couldn't discern whether it was from pleasure or abhorrence. Whatever it was, he knew he had stepped over the line and pushed their friendship to a place it was never meant to be. He'd been determined to keep his feelings under control, and he'd failed. He wasn't ready to open his heart. *This was a mistake.*

With a muttered "Bye, Sophie," he left.

The walk home was bitterly cold, as if his confusion weren't misery enough.

Hours later, he sat in an old Morris chair and stared into the fire while he struggled to reconcile his head and his heart. His psychology degree hadn't been of much use to him since graduation, except to convince him that he was depressed. Since losing his business, he'd lost the ability to enjoy aspects of life that he used to relish. He barely thought about getting on his bike anymore, although the snow would have prohibited riding anyhow. He didn't care about what the future held for him. All the plans and dreams he had cherished and worked diligently for had been senselessly ruined. Hopelessness over-whelmed him for most of his waking moments—except when he was with Sophie. With her, he felt almost alive.

As flames burned their pattern through the logs in the fire, Cole went through it over and over again, but it always led to one irrefutable fact. He had nothing to give her except disappointment.

11

Sophie didn't sleep well. She could still feel that kiss.

From the start, she'd felt different about Cole. But in life, there were interesting people—attractive people—all around. That didn't mean they belonged with each other, especially now, when the timing was wrong. Sophie had come to the mountains to find peace so she could think clearly about what to do in the new year. A romantic entanglement would undercut all her efforts. She couldn't feel peaceful when her heart kept skipping beats.

But she liked Cole, so she muted that voice in her head that kept sending her warnings, and she spent time with him. Their day at the tree farm had been almost normal—better than normal—which was why she'd let down her guard. She'd known he was going to kiss her. They'd stood too close and too still for too long. And she'd wanted to kiss him. Even knowing that she would regret it, she'd wanted that kiss more than anything else. But she would pay a price for that kiss.

Her phone chimed to signal an incoming text.

Cole: *Good morning.*

Sophie: *Good morning.*

Cole: *Are you up?*

Sophie: *It's 11:00. Yeah, I'm up.*

Cole: *How 'bout coffee?*

Sophie: *Sure. I just made some. Come on over.*

Cole: *Okay.*

Five minutes later, Sophie set down two mugs and joined Cole at the table that overlooked Cedar Creek. Following an awkward pause, they both started talking at once.

Cole said, "You first."

"No, you called me. You go first."

Cole nodded. "I really like you." Even though he didn't say *but*, the regret in his eyes was enough.

Sophie sighed with relief. "Oh, thank God. I feel the same way. We got ahead of ourselves."

He nodded emphatically. "If we were at different points in our lives..."

"Things might be different."

"Exactly."

Sophie stared at the creek. Water rushed over the

rocks and made its way along its cedar-lined path through the snow. "We both came here to escape."

Cole looked wistful. "And we've done it. But neither of us is ready."

Getting it out in the open felt good. "It's a frying-pan-fire situation." And yet, as relieved as she was, she couldn't help wishing it could be different. "We should be friends."

"We are, and I like that about us." Cole's eyes crinkled as he smiled. Something about that always charmed her. His smile relaxed. "Maybe someday..."

"Maybe." Sophie relaxed. They agreed, and no hearts had been broken. What a waste it was, though, when they both seemed so suited for each other. They could have been perfect together.

Cole grinned. "You're a force to behold with a bow saw though."

"Oh, yeah? Wait till my new chainsaw arrives." When his jaw predictably dropped, she laughed. "Just kidding. I'm saving that till after I've mastered the snowblower."

"I have every faith that you will." He nodded, but with a glint in his eye.

"We did have a good day on the tree farm. And you got a tree. See what a better person you are for having known me?" She laughed.

His smile faded. "I am. You're a good friend to have."

A magnetic force tugged at her heart, but Sophie held her ground. "You too."

Their eyes locked and made lies of their promises of friendship. Sophie wanted to reach over and touch his hand. Just a touch. That was all she wanted, to be just a little bit closer. The air was so still that she couldn't take it anymore. She stood. "How 'bout a coffee warm-up?"

Distractedly, he looked up. "Sure."

Sophie refilled their mugs and sat down. "It looks like good weather today for the Christmas Market." She looked down. She wished she hadn't mentioned the market. It sounded like she was hinting, when instead, she was doing her best to think of anything else but the two of them.

He looked as unsure of himself as she was of herself. "We could still do things together, couldn't we? I mean, I don't want to make things awkward. Dammit. Like saying that didn't just make things awkward. I just want to go back to yesterday."

The awkwardness wasn't the worst. The worst was feeling they'd lost everything in the bargain. Sophie could not let that happen. Doing her best to seem normal again, she looked at her watch. "Well, if we're going to go, we'd better get started. All the best stuff will be picked over by noon, and I've still got a lot of Christmas shopping to do."

Cole's whole countenance brightened. "I'll drive in case we get something too big for your car."

Sophie laughed. "When I said a lot of Christmas shopping, I didn't mean enough to fill the bed of your truck."

"Better safe than sorry."

They were both smiling. It wasn't quite normal, but it was close enough for now. Sophie said, "I need to get ready. I'll meet you at your place in twenty minutes."

He looked into her eyes. "I'll be there."

He left smiling, then Sophie closed the door gently and took a moment. They'd weathered a storm. But she was already having second thoughts about their friendship arrangement. The guy had just said he was looking forward to a holiday market. That was a guy worth hanging on to.

Sophie hadn't done any of her Christmas shopping, so she wandered through the market with a list and a mission. She'd always admired anyone who got all their shopping done early. She was never that person. Despite her best efforts to beat the rush, the market was already teeming with people when they got there. In the wild sea of shoppers, they were swept into the currents, which led them to kiosks of holiday gifts and treats that they might not have found on their own. At times, the holiday spirit manifested in Christmas shoppers in unusual ways, but Cole took it in stride when an elderly woman determined to defy the laws of physics by occupying Cole's space in line gave his kidney a poke with her walker.

Two hours later, Sophie was thrilled to have found something for everyone on her list, except one. At one end of the market stood a booth offering sleigh rides. Sophie was about to suggest they go on one when Cole went to the booth and signed up. They waited for their turn at a hot chocolate stand.

Cole asked, "Have you ever been on a sleigh ride?"

"No, but it sounds very..." *Romantic? No.* "Fun."

When their turn came, Cole held out his hand to help Sophie climb onto the sleigh. Then he joined her, and off they went. Sophie had been right on both counts. It was romantic *and* fun.

The temperature was just below freezing, cold enough to put color in their cheeks. As they reached a turning point, the driver paused to let them take in the view of Cedar Creek cutting a twisting path through a blanket of snow. The skating pond was full of couples and families with young children. On Main Street, shoppers flowed in and out of the shops. As the driver headed back toward the market, Sophie's heart was full. There was joy in the air, and beside her, Cole looked just as happy as she felt. This was how Christmas should always be.

With their arms weighed down with shopping bags, they walked back to the truck. When they'd loaded their bags and climbed into their seats, Sophie turned to Cole. "That was a perfect day. And here's a Christmas miracle. My shopping is done."

"Mine too. Just in time."

For the first time, a thought occurred to Sophie. "I haven't asked you what you're doing for Christmas. My family's coming to the cottage. Why don't you come over?"

He looked genuinely touched by the gesture, although she meant it as more. Whatever awkwardness lingered between them, she would never want to leave him alone in his cabin on Christmas Day.

"Thanks. I appreciate the invite. I'm actually going home Christmas Eve to be with my family."

"Oh, that's great."

"Yeah, it's just a quick trip, but I'm looking forward to it."

Sophie was glad to hear that he would be with family on Christmas, but she felt a twinge of disappointment that he would be away—which was silly. He would only be gone for a couple of days. *Friends can go days without seeing each other. And that's what we are. We're just friends.*

On the way home, Sophie's phone rang. Cole didn't want to eavesdrop, but they were inches apart in a truck. He couldn't avoid hearing her half—and sometimes the other—of the phone conversation.

"Ellen? Hi."

Silence followed, then she said, "Our jobs?" She looked puzzled.

Unfortunately, the need to maneuver his truck along a winding road forced him to look away and keep his eyes on the road.

Sophie did more listening than talking. When she did respond, it was monosyllabic.

The call ended, and Sophie fixed expressionless eyes straight ahead. "I can't believe it."

She had Cole's attention.

"It's just talk at this point, but the defunding isn't going as well as they'd planned. There's been a huge spike in violent crime, and response time is down. There are rumblings of change, but I think it's just wishful thinking. Any change would require a city council vote. Still, there's an outside chance I could get my job back."

Cole wasn't as surprised by the news as he was by Sophie's reaction to it. "You're not considering it, are you?"

"I don't know. It's not the same city I used to love."

Cole pulled into Sophie's driveway and parked. He considered whether to voice his opinion. "I'd just hate to see you walk back into a situation that volatile."

"I know, but I felt like I was making a difference. I miss that."

Cole tried, but he couldn't get the image of his ruined store out of his mind. "There must be a better place for you to make a difference."

"Maybe, but I don't know where."

The anger he thought he'd left back in the city rose to the surface. "Come on, Sophie. Anywhere would be better than that."

Sophie said, "It's better than hiding out here in the woods."

Her words cut deep. But she was right. That was what he was doing. Until now, he'd been sure it was helping. He'd reset his life, and he was recharging. He thought Sophie understood. Maybe that was what hurt the most.

Sophie shut her eyes for a moment. "I'm sorry. That's not what I meant."

"Isn't it?"

"No, I just... I love it here, but you can't live on vacation."

"Vacation? I never thought of it that way. For me, it felt more like being buried in grief over the loss of my hopes and dreams for the business I'd worked so hard to build—and the agonizing feeling of helplessness while the world around me went mad. But I guess you could call it a vacation."

"Cole—" She shook her head while she seemed to be searching for words.

"It's late. Good night, Sophie." He could see he'd upset her, and he knew he would regret it. He just couldn't feel it now.

"Good night." She gathered her shopping bags, got out of the truck as quickly as she could, then fled to her door. Once she was safely inside, Cole backed the truck out and pulled into his driveway.

12

Sophie finished her housecleaning and moved on to cooking. Everything was clean and smelled good for the holidays.

Five days had gone by without Cole. His truck had been gone from his driveway until this morning. When Sophie got up, it was there.

After some coffee for fortification, she went over to his cabin and knocked. He answered the door with a look on his face that was worse than anger. He was cold and almost indifferent.

"Cole, I'm sorry. I spoke without thinking."

"It's okay. I may have overreacted."

His reserved manner made her feel worse. "Can we find a way past this?"

He hesitated. "I'm sorry, Sophie."

She was stunned. As vague as he had been before, his clarity at that moment was painful. "Just like that?" She searched his eyes, but they were distant and cold.

It was almost a shrug, but his shoulders lifted slightly as if to say, "It's no use."

"Cole, we're friends."

"I can't be."

"Can't be friends?"

For the first time since answering the door, he looked straight into her eyes. "No. Not just like that at all."

"I don't understand."

Cole's eyes softened, but more from pain than affection. "You were right. I am hiding out in the woods."

Sophie had never regretted words more. "I've been hiding out too. I just meant that we have to come out of hiding at some point."

"But you're ready to go back, and that's good. I was wrong to resent you for that. I think what really stung was how it highlighted the fact that I'm not. I'm not ready, and I might never be. But I'm content to stay here."

"That's okay. None of that means we can't be friends."

"I can't." Cole looked away. "I should've told you from the start I was broken. It's not permanent—at least I hope not. I'm just not in any shape to offer anything to a relationship."

"Not even friendship?"

"I can't do friendship right now."

"Cole..." She stopped herself. There was nothing to say short of begging, so she turned and walked back to her cottage.

She would not let this ruin her Christmas. She'd planned an amazing visit for her family. But with five days to go before they arrived, she still had a long to-do list. With all the shopping, cooking, and wrapping of presents, she had plenty to keep her mind off Cole. He'd never been a part of that plan anyway, since he would be away with his family. She just hoped he would leave soon. With no reminders of him, she could set aside the whole issue and enjoy Christmas with her family. She was determined.

Sophie delved deep into baking therapy, making batches of cookie dough to freeze. Her family would have fresh homemade cookies throughout their visit. When the last dish was dried and put away, Sophie hung up her dish towel. If she could design her own piece of heaven, it would look and smell just like this. Ignoring the Cole-sized ache in her heart, she fixed herself a hot chocolate, put a log on the fire, and turned on the TV to watch a Christmas movie.

While she scanned the directory, she caught the weather report. With all the cleaning and cooking—and Cole—she hadn't turned on the TV in a day and a half. A big snowstorm was headed up the coast, with storm watches and warnings and some serious snowfall projections. But what got her attention was the mention of road closures. They hadn't closed yet, and they might not at all, but the fact that the news report mentioned it was enough to cause her some concern. Of course, up in the mountains in the dead of winter, storms were inevitable. But the possibility of becoming stranded was suddenly real.

She muted the TV and called home. Her father answered. When she asked if he'd heard about the weather, he said, "How could I not? It's all they've been talking about for days."

Sophie said, "What if you can't get here for Christmas?"

"We are not driving up for five days. They'll have the roads cleared by then. Relax, honey. You know how it is with those TV weather people. Every blip on the radar is a snowmageddon event. They scare you just enough to keep you tuned in to their channel. Half the time, these storms are just nonevents that blow over."

"It's the other half I'm worried about."

"That's my little worrier."

There it was. At some point in their conversations, she reverted in his eyes to nine-year-old Sophie. But he did have a point. She was worried. Her perfect Christmas depended on having family here with her.

Her father continued, "I promise we'll be there. Just make sure you're prepared to be snowed in—just in case."

"Thanks, Daddy."

"Oh, gotta go. We're on our way out for some last-minute shopping, and your mother is pointing at her watch with that look."

"Okay. Love you!"

"I love you too. See you soon!"

"Okay, bye."

Sophie set down her phone and looked out at the creek. Not a snowflake in sight, and she willed it to stay that way.

Sophie warmed up her hot chocolate, turned up the TV volume, and decided on a Christmas movie to watch. She had managed to stay busy enough to avoid thoughts of Cole, but all it took was one idle moment for her thoughts to stray.

It had all gone so terribly wrong, and she still didn't understand why. Cole had reacted so strongly to the idea of her going back to her old job that she'd started to doubt her own judgment. Maybe he had a point. It didn't matter what sort of difference she made if her job could come and go on a whim. But it wasn't as if it were personal. Decisions had been made, and she'd been collateral damage.

Even if she did go back, it wouldn't be the same, though. She used to feel so sure of her place in the world. She was proud that, in her small way, she added value to her community. But the community didn't seem to agree. The city had changed. Maybe it was time to reconsider her options.

At dusk in winter, the silvery snow slowly darkened to gray, until the tips of the evergreen branches caught the last glimpses of sun before it dipped beyond view. Taking its place, the warm glow from cabin windows peeked through the trees, making the world feel still and warm.

Cole's lights were on. He walked past one of the windows, and Sophie wished he would walk past it again. She missed him.

Tossed about by the wind, a few snow flurries danced in the air. A few minutes later, a steady snowfall was underway. Sophie turned on the outdoor floodlight to see it more clearly. It was her favorite kind of snow—big fluffy flakes. Having lost interest in her movie, she decided this was a perfect night to curl up by the fire and read a book.

First, she put a couple of her homemade Christmas cookies on a plate, poured herself a glass of milk, and got out her favorite from a chest of her grandmother's quilts. Once settled, she took one last look at the snow falling outside the window then began to read.

One chapter into her book, everything went dark. Other than the amber glow from the fire, the cottage was the kind of dark it could only be in the country. She sat for a moment while her circumstances set in. Then she took a deep breath. Her grandmother's furnace required power to run, so her only source of heat now was the woodstove. She would need more logs to get through the night, so she shrugged on her jacket and gloves and went out to the woodshed. She made twice as many trips as she probably needed, but she didn't want to open the door and lose heat any more than she had to, so she stocked up for at least twenty-four hours. With the wood-fetching done, there was little else left to do. She could read on her phone, but she didn't want to run down the battery in case she might need it for an emergency call. So she did an Abe Lincoln and read by the firelight.

With the slight adjustment of adding a second quilt, she was reading comfortably when a loud knock on the door startled her. Leaving the warmth of her quilt, she went to the door. After her last conversation with Cole, she knew it couldn't be him, so she stood quietly deciding whether to answer it. *What if it's a crazed woodsman?*

"Sophie, it's Cole! Open the door!"

She opened the door, ushered him in, and shut the door quickly. While he stomped the snow from his boots, she said, "Are you okay?"

"Yeah, I'm fine. I was worried about you."

"The power went out, but I'm fine."

Cole brushed the snow from his jacket. "I thought you might need help starting your generator."

"I have a generator?"

His mouth twitched, but he suppressed a smile. "That's what I figured. You have one. I saw it when I was putting away the snowblower."

"Oh, wow. And you know how to work it?"

"I think so. We had one at my house, growing up. This isn't the same kind, but it can't be all that different."

They seemed to have a tacit agreement to act as though things were normal between them, completely ignoring how they'd left things. Survival was the important matter at hand, so they focused their attention on the generator. By the light of Cole's kerosene lantern, they both went out to the garage. Sophie held the lantern while Cole examined the generator and nodded. That seemed like a good sign. Then he stood and faced Sophie.

"The good news is, it's not very old, which makes me think it might work."

"That's great. Then let's start her up."

"The bad news is, you don't have any fuel."

"Oh, great."

"When I say you don't have any fuel, I should qualify that. If worse came to worst, you could siphon some out of your car. But I'd save that as a last resort."

"Good call. That sounds gross."

Cole winced. "I wouldn't recommend it. For the next storm, you might want to stock up on a couple cans of gas, just in case."

Sophie exhaled. "Right. Good to know. Okay, well, I guess it's the pioneer life for me."

They stepped back outside, then Cole pulled down the garage door. They crunched through ankle-deep snow to get back to the house, where Sophie paused at the steps leading up to her door. "Cole, I'm sorry."

He shook his head. "No. It was my fault. You touched a raw nerve, and I lashed out at you. You didn't deserve it."

Relief washed over Sophie. "It wasn't fair—what I said about hiding out in the woods."

"But I am. I've always thought of myself as proactive. I'm not wired to be a victim, so the thought of cowering in the woods made me feel guilty."

"I never said 'cowering.'"

"I know. I just translated it to that. Anyway, you don't owe me an apology. It wasn't your fault."

Sophie felt relieved to be talking with Cole again. She looked up at the sky, but clouds obscured the stars. "You got me thinking about my own situation. I thought I wanted to go back because part of me wants to rewind everything and get back to normal. But there is no more normal. I think I've finally faced up to that fact."

This was the part where they both said goodbye. Sophie looked about. "It's so peaceful here."

Cole nodded and looked toward his cabin.

"And a little scary."

It was too dark to read Cole's expression. "Would you like me to—" He gestured toward the door.

"Please!"

Once inside and settled on the sofa near the fire, Sophie said, "You didn't leave a blazing fire unattended, did you?"

"No, I banked what was left of the fire in my woodstove and came over to check on you first."

"Thanks." She had missed that smile. She had missed him. But they were together. Everything felt all right now.

He pointed at her book. "What are we reading?"

Warmed by the quilts and the fire, Cole took the first turn reading by firelight. "'Marley was dead, to begin with. There is no doubt whatever about that.'" He slipped his arm about her shoulders and continued.

13

Cole woke with Sophie in his arms. They'd fallen asleep reading by the fire. Only embers remained in the fireplace, so without waking Sophie, Cole slipped away to add logs to the fire. After he'd gotten the fire going again, he turned to find Sophie awake.

"Good morning." She sat up, looking sleepy.

With fresh logs on the fire, Cole smiled and sat back down beside her. Being together felt easy again, as if they'd always been meant to be like this. But they still stood at the edge of friendship, unsure of which way to go next. He put his arm about her shoulders while they watched the logs catch fire.

The boiler turned on, and Sophie's mood brightened. "Yay! We've got power again! I can face the day now. Which reminds me, my grandmother's arriving today for an overnight visit. She's got some business in town, but we're meeting for dinner. Why don't you join us?"

"I can't." Part of him wished that he could, but it was better this way. Even though they were friends—who sat with their arms around each other—meeting anyone in her family would raise all sorts of questions and expectations that were better left for another time. Even so, he might have been tempted to accept her invitation if he hadn't had other plans. "I've got to go home for a couple of days and take care of some things."

Sophie nodded. "Oh, okay. Well, I'll see you when you get back." She looked into his eyes, and all his feelings of friendship just flew out the window.

They nearly kissed, but instead, Cole rested his forehead on hers. "We keep finding ourselves here at this place we're not ready to be."

Sophie looked away. "I'm sorry. I know that you just want to be friends. I hear you, but then I see you and—I don't know what I'm doing."

He shook his head and took her face in his hands, then he kissed her. Sophie put her arms around his neck and pressed closer. Cole said softly, "Apparently, I suck at friendship." And he kissed her again.

Sophie didn't want it to stop, but when he gently pulled back, she put her palms on his chest. "I want this."

"I do too." He leaned closer, but Sophie kept him at bay.

"But—"

Cole blinked slowly. "I think I hate that word."

"Me too, but..."

Cole exhaled and leaned his back against the sofa while Sophie continued.

"You're not ready. You're the one who said that, and I trust you."

"Sophie, I'm a mess. I'm confused about everything in my life—except you. And I don't want to lose you before we know what we could be."

"You won't lose me. Let's just take a breath and give it some time."

He looked into her eyes. "You're right, but I'm not gonna like it."

When she smiled, her eyes sparkled. It was all he could do not to kiss her again. But he knew she was right. They needed to slow down. A few days away might be just what they needed.

Softly, she said, "How 'bout some coffee?"

"Coffee sounds good."

They talked and laughed over breakfast, then Cole looked out the window. "I can't believe it's still snowing. The roads won't be great, so I'd better get going."

Sophie fixed him a travel mug of coffee and

walked him to the door. "Thanks for staying last night. It's dark and scary out here alone in the woods." She smiled, but he knew she meant it.

"I didn't like the idea of leaving you here without power, so I'm glad it's back on."

"I'll be fine now, and my grandmother will be here soon. She knows people in town she could call if anything happens." She smiled warmly. "Which it won't."

"Good." He drew her into his arms. "I'll be back in a couple of days." He kissed her on the forehead. He was on his way out the door when her grandmother pulled into the driveway.

Sophie introduced Cole. She could practically read her grandmother's mind as she shook Cole's hand and smiled.

Sophie said, "Cole was just leaving."

"It was nice to meet you, Mrs. Furnell."

"Kate."

Cole smiled. "Kate."

Sophie couldn't decide who was more charmed, her grandmother or Cole. When he was gone, her grandmother said with an air of approval, "He's good-looking."

Sophie's knee-jerk reaction was to act as though she hadn't noticed his looks, but no one, especially her grandmother, would ever believe that. Cole had the kind of confidence without being arrogant that people noticed when he entered a room, and yes, he was good-looking. *Thanks, Grandma Kate.*

Her grandmother eyed Sophie without saying anything. She just waited.

Finally, unable to take any more, Sophie played along. "What?"

Grandma Kate shrugged. "Oh, nothing." With a knowing smile, her grandmother pulled her overnight bag from the car.

"Here, let me get that."

Sophie put her grandmother's bag in her bedroom then joined her grandmother in the kitchen for some tea. As she dipped her tea bag in the water, Grandma Kate said, "Cole seems nice."

"Yes, he is."

"And very good-looking."

Nodding, Sophie said, "Yes, I believe you mentioned that. He is very nice and good-looking."

"And single?"

"Yes."

"Hmm."

Sophie thought hard for another subject—any subject. "So I thought we might have dinner in the village."

Relieved to have left the topic of Cole behind, they chatted about family and her grandmother's friends, then her grandmother left for an appointment.

Sophie arrived at her grandmother's favorite place to eat in town, an old historic inn. As often happened, while they waited for their table, her grandmother saw people she knew and caught up on the news about mutual friends. Through her eyes, Sophie gained a new perspective of the village and the warmth of its people. She was falling in love with Cedar Creek, which was going to make it harder to leave in the spring.

As they walked into the dining room, Sophie felt the warmth from a huge marble fireplace. Draped on the mantel and throughout the room, Christmas greenery and red plaid bows lent the room a Christmassy charm.

They talked over wine. To put it mildly, her grandmother was an interesting woman who had led an unusual life. Widowed in her forties, she'd spent much of the following decade traveling independently, sometimes staying for weeks at a time tucked away in charming places unvisited by tourists. Her favorite souvenirs were the stories she'd brought back and the friends she had made. Although she'd slowed down in recent years, she was every bit as lively and interesting to talk with as ever. Their dinner was no exception.

Once home, the two stayed up late, talking and laughing. It was strange how, as much as she loved both her parents, Sophie connected with her grandmother in a way she didn't with her parents. Grandma Kate and Sophie were so much alike in their interests and their views of the world. It was almost as if the genes that controlled personality and interests seemed to have skipped a generation and landed with Sophie. Whatever the reason, when the two got together, they were never at a loss for something to discuss or debate.

At one point, Grandma Kate grew serious. "How are you?"

Sophie gave her grandmother a positive smile. "I'm good."

Her grandmother leaned closer. "No, how *are* you?"

She always saw through Sophie. "I'm still trying to figure it out—'it' being my life."

"Life does that to you, but sometimes it's for a good reason. And if it isn't, then you just have to fix it," she said matter-of-factly, which was easy for her. She was happy with her life.

"It's not always easy."

Grandma Kate lifted her eyebrows. "Oh, I didn't say it was easy. It can be miserably hard."

A pang of guilt nagged at Sophie. Her grandmother had lost a husband, so Sophie had no business complaining that life was hard. "I'm sorry. I didn't mean to whine."

"It's not whining. I asked you." And that was what Sophie loved about Grandma Kate. She made Sophie feel like a better person than she was.

Sophie said, "I guess I'm still angry because I thought I had my life figured out. I loved my job and my life, and they took it all from me."

A gentle smile spread to her grandmother's eyes. "You can spend your whole life being angry at 'them,' but the thing about that is, you just hurt yourself."

"I know. What I don't know is how to stop."

"Being angry?"

"Yes! It wasn't my fault that I lost my job."

"Of course it wasn't! The world has gone a bit mad, but you can't control that."

"So what do I do?" Sophie was frustrated—not with her grandmother, but with herself.

Grandma Kate spoke patiently. "Sophie, it's Christmas. What is Christmas about?"

She felt like she was taking a test and failing. Her mind raced. "Christmas trees, gifts—giving." She looked at her grandmother, hoping she might be getting closer to the answer. She wasn't. She tried again and went for the obvious. "The birth of Christ."

"Why?"

Of course, Sophie knew the answer from child-hood Sunday school classes. "Salvation." That was all well and good. She'd done all the church things. "Grandma, I get it. I believe that Christ died for my sins so I'll be forgiven and have eternal life. But what about real life?"

"Forgive. It's all about forgiving."

"Forgiving won't get me my job back."

"You've got every right to be angry about losing your job. It wasn't fair."

"I know!"

Her grandmother took Sophie's hands in hers. "You can't change the past, but being bitter about it can ruin your future. When you feel stuck and don't know which way to turn, sometimes the best thing to do is to forgive those who have wronged you. If you can forgive, it will free you and make room for hope. And that's something you can build a life on."

Sophie furrowed her eyebrows. "I guess..."

"Christmas is a time for miracles."

Sophie tried to smile through her frustration. "Sounds great. I'm ready for mine."

Her grandmother's eyes sparkled. "Forgiveness is a miracle you have the power to make happen."

As nice as it sounded, her grandmother came from another era. Today's world was no longer the kind, gentle world her grandmother had grown up in.

But Sophie loved her and wasn't about to argue the point, so she gave her a hug. "Thanks, Grandma."

In the morning, they had breakfast, then Sophie walked her grandmother out to the car.

Grandma Kate hugged Sophie. "I think I'll stop on my way through the village and visit a couple of friends for a quick hello and to wish them a merry Christmas."

"That sounds nice."

Before getting into her car, Grandma Kate turned and leaned on the car door. "Oh, and that Cole? Hang on to him. He's a keeper!"

Sophie's jaw dropped, but she recovered. "Grandma, we're not..."

Her grandmother winked. "Goodbye, honey."

Her grandmother backed out of the driveway and drove off, leaving Sophie to mull over what she and Cole were or were not.

14

Sophie finished washing the dishes, then she sat on the window seat and stared out at the creek. Since the previous day, she'd been stewing over something her grandmother had said. Forgiveness was easy when it was something small. If someone cut her off in traffic or said something rude, she could forgive them eventually. But she'd lost her job and her apartment, and the city she'd once loved had changed. She knew there would be other jobs, and she would rebuild her life. But so much of the life she'd known had been destroyed, and not even the city leaders seemed to know how to rebuild it.

If she followed her grandmother's advice, she would forgive them. At the moment, she couldn't, but she would definitely put that on her to-do list. Maybe later, when her emotional wounds and her bank account healed, she would be able to manage a little forgiveness.

With that topic dispensed with, she began wondering what to do next. *Maybe Grandma Kate was right. Just thinking about forgiveness has made room for thoughts of the future.* When the holidays were over, she might be ready to move forward. Taking a step at a time, things looked doable. In fact, a change might even improve her professional life. She couldn't pinpoint what was different, but the fog seemed to clear. She could see herself applying for jobs—and she would get one. After that, she would save up for an apartment. She had done it before. There was no reason she couldn't do it again. She still didn't like having to start all over from scratch, but there was no point in dwelling on that.

It wasn't even the new year, but on a whim, she looked through some job listings on an employment website. Two of them looked like a good fit, so she applied. It was a step. She felt good about that. Last on the list was her personal life. That would have to wait at the bottom of the list next to forgiveness— which made two miracles that she would need in her life.

She really liked Cole, but they always seemed to be out of sync. She'd always thought people who were truly meant for each other wouldn't have to battle such obstacles. They would simply fall in love, be together, and walk through the figurative door to their future. She and Cole weren't together, at least not in that way, so there was no elusive door to their future. She convinced herself it didn't matter. They were good together for now. It would end eventually, but eventually was a long way away. Sophie would keep things in perspective, then move on with no hard feelings when it was over. People did that all the time.

Sophie's phone signaled an incoming text. She hoped her grandmother hadn't taken a wrong turn and gotten lost. Although, for a woman who had traveled half the globe on her own, driving home would be child's play for her. To Sophie's surprise, the text was from Cole.

Cole: *I caught some fish. How 'bout dinner?*

Sophie: *Okay. When?*

Cole: *How's seven?*

Sophie: *Okay.*

Cole: *See you then—at my place.*

Sophie: *Okay. See you later.*

Sophie stared at her phone screen. *His place? Okay.* It was dinner. Friends had dinner. *Or it could be a date.* Setting her phone down, she stared at the lacy snow-dusted trees outside her window and smiled.

Cole spent the afternoon clearing carpentry and painting debris, then he cleaned the house. While he worked, he thought back on his morning. He did his best thinking when he was fishing. There was something cleansing about being in nature. It was simple and pure. For that moment in time, he was part of the wilderness. The sounds and sensations of nature had a way of rebalancing priorities and granting some moments of peace in a world full of chaos.

During a quick break for a glass of water, Cole surveyed his handiwork. He couldn't have pinpointed the moment it happened. He'd set out merely to freshen up the cabin to make it more habitable. But as he delved into the project, his thoughts shifted from cosmetic repairs to complete renovation. Inherent in that was the assumption that he would be staying. He had made no commitment. He was free to pack up and move any time. There was nothing to stop him from moving back to the city and trying to rebuild the life he had lost. But as the days went by and he drove into town to go shopping, he got to know people. He would chat as he checked out his building supplies or his groceries, and he felt a sense of belonging he hadn't expected.

There must have been a moment when he knew

he would stay, but it crept up so gradually that he'd never noticed. One day, he imagined his future and saw Cedar Creek at the center of it. The more he envisioned his future in Cedar Creek, the less broken he felt by the past. Nothing could erase the devastation of watching his business being destroyed, but reliving the past was a burden holding him back from his new life. And that new life was in Cedar Creek.

As Cole put the cleaning supplies back in the closet, his thoughts turned to his upcoming evening with Sophie. This would be their first proper date, although he hadn't made that clear to Sophie. He'd been packing his fishing gear into the back of his truck when the thought came to him on a whim. A morning of fishing had left him in a good mood—too good not to share. So he texted Sophie and invited her over for dinner.

He hadn't defined it as such, but he considered it a date. Still, whether or not it turned out that way was up to Sophie. They'd crossed the bounds of mere friendship without firmly planting their feet on the other side. To be safe, ambivalence seemed like the best way to go. If the evening went well, it could seamlessly move into a more date-like situation. If not —no harm, no foul. Either way, he wanted to show off the work he had done in the cabin. Paint was a magical substance. His cabin looked fresh and warm.

A stone fireplace that reached up past the beams to the ceiling didn't hurt, and the refinished floors were now gleaming. It still had a long way to go, but the cabin was looking increasingly warm and inviting.

Not long after seven, Sophie arrived with a bottle of wine and a basket of freshly baked herb-seasoned biscuits to go with the fish. Cole proudly took her on a tour of the cabin and showed her the work he had done. It was a small cabin, which made for a very brief tour, but Sophie's eyes lit up as she walked through it.

"It's perfect. Its rustic charm married to modern touches. And you did all this yourself!"

Cole shrugged. "It's a work in progress." Despite being a little embarrassed, he enjoyed her approval. "Let's crack open this wine, and then I'll get to work on the fish."

When he poured only one glass, Sophie said, "Oh, you're not a wine person, are you?"

"Oh, I'll have some wine with dinner, but I can't grill without a beer in my hand." He offered a helpless smile, and she laughed.

Armed with a beer in his jacket pocket and a platter of fish, Cole headed outside to the smoker. "Make yourself at home. I'll be back in a few."

While he waited for the fish, he took a drink from his beer and glanced inside at Sophie. She was perusing a small stack of books and magazines he'd left on the coffee table. After the recent power outage, he realized he hadn't brought enough non-screen entertainment, so he'd grabbed a few items from the grocery store book racks. He liked seeing her in his cabin. She didn't seem like a guest. She fit there, and he felt comfortable with her. He wasn't sure if that was a good thing or not. He didn't need to decide at the moment, so he turned his thoughts elsewhere. The fish needed attention. The rest would take care of itself.

Over dinner, they talked easily. Perhaps that was what confused him. Sometimes he felt like they were friends. The thought of making it more added pressure that could ruin this delicate balance they had. But then there were times, like right now, when the glow of the candlelight and warmth from the fire lit the planes of her face and caught the light in her eyes. In moments like this, he just wanted to kiss her.

While Cole was caught up in the glow of desire, Sophie sipped wine and grinned. "By the way, Grandma Kate loves you!"

So much for the glow of desire. Cole laughed. "She spent all of two minutes with me."

Nodding, Sophie said, "She's a good judge of character."

"I'm not sure I want to be the kind of guy grand-mothers love."

Sophie laughed. "There are worse things to be."

Cole grimaced. "I always wondered what it would be like to be a James Dean kind of guy, but I wound up like Jimmy Stewart." Cole slumped piti-fully in his chair.

Sophie's face lit up. "I love Jimmy Stewart!"

"Really?" He straightened his posture as he began to rethink his self-image.

"In the phone scene from *It's a Wonderful Life*—when he kisses Donna Reed, that's just the best movie kiss ever. Except for *Reds*—no... I'm pretty sure that's an embrace, so it doesn't count."

"I need to watch more movies—and maybe take notes." He laughed, but Sophie didn't laugh with him.

Instead, her eyes softened, and she gazed into his. "You don't need to take notes."

Cole felt like climbing over the table and kissing her right then and there, letting fish bones and tartar sauce land where they may. It took effort, but he refrained.

Sophie averted her eyes as the conversation all but halted. They finished eating and stood. When they were done clearing the table, Sophie set down her plates by the sink and turned.

Cole took her hand and drew her close. "I don't want to be friends anymore." He kissed her. All he could think of, besides how soft Sophie's lips felt, was Jimmy Stewart. He really wished she hadn't mentioned that kiss. It was his own fault. He was the one who'd brought up Jimmy Stewart.

Somehow, he managed to drive the image from his mind, and he kissed her again. This time, it was all about Cole kissing Sophie.

15

Sophie poured her first cup of coffee of the day and sat at the kitchen island. The warmth of a blush came to her cheeks as she thought about Cole. Leaving last night had been hard. She'd done it, but not without some Herculean willpower. So much about Cole was perfect. When they'd first met, he'd been through some hard times, but he seemed to be working through things. Their relationship hadn't begun smoothly, but their feelings were real. Sophie had faith in those feelings. Cedar Creek was a good place to heal. Even in the stillness of winter, the rhythm of nature made the rest seem so simple.

A knock at the door tore her from her thoughts.

"Cole!" She was as surprised as she was happy to see him.

He leaned on the doorframe. "Is it too early?"

"No, come on in! I just made some coffee."

He sat down at the island and leaned on his elbows, gazing at her with boyish charm. "That was going to be my excuse—that I ran out of coffee. To be honest, I just wanted to see you."

Sophie's heart filled with joy. Overwhelmed, she turned to hide her reaction and took her time getting a mug from the cupboard. Doing her best to hold her emotions in check, she poured his coffee.

He took a drink then leaned forward. "Let's do something!"

"Okay. Like what?" As much as she enjoyed his enthusiasm, it was a little disconcerting. This was a different Cole from the one she thought she knew.

"I don't know. You're the Christmas fanatic."

"Well, I wouldn't say that exactly. I mean, I love Christmas—"

"Because it makes you happy."

Sophie wasn't quite following him.

He went on. "So I want to be happy with you."

Half amused and half confused, she said, "Okay. Give me a minute to think."

He leaned back and sipped his coffee, looking completely content.

Sophie's phone rang. "Grandma Kate, hi!"

"Honey, I've got a favor to ask."

"Okay."

"I am so sorry to spoil all your plans, but the property manager's new assistant made a mistake, and she's booked the cottage for the holidays."

"Oh." Sophie wasn't sure what she'd expected when her grandmother asked for a favor, but that wasn't it. "So you want me to leave?"

Cole looked up.

"Honey, I feel terrible about this, but... yes. It's just for the week—no, actually..."

Sophie waited while her grandmother counted the days to herself.

"It's ten days. From the twenty-third until after the new year. The second, to be exact."

"Oh. Okay." Sophie stared at the fridge and thought through all her Christmas meal plans. She wouldn't have her magical Cedar Creek setting, but the rest of her Christmas plans could happen at home. "Sure. I'll just pack up the baked goods and groceries and do the cooking at home. And I'll stay home a few days longer."

Grandma Kate sighed with relief. "I was hoping you'd say that. I'm so sorry. The poor girl is new. It was an honest mistake. And it's Christmas."

The part of Sophie that wanted to be annoyed found it difficult when her grandmother put it like that. "That's okay. So when do I need to be out?"

"Well, it would help if you left by tomorrow morning so the housekeeping crew could get in."

"Okay."

"Honey, I'm sorry. On the plus side, I'll be at your parents' house when you get there, so I'll expect you to put me to work in the kitchen."

"Oh, good! We'll have fun!"

"I can't wait. And you're stuck with me until the new year."

"That sounds great."

Grandma Kate said, "I'll let you go, but be thinking of things you might like to do between Christmas and New Year's. For starters, shopping and lunch. Maybe movies?"

Sophie smiled. "I like the way you think!"

"Good. See you soon."

"Bye, Grandma." She set down her phone and looked at Cole. "So I'm leaving—"

"Tomorrow. I heard."

"I'll be gone until January second."

Cole hid his disappointment almost completely, but Sophie recognized it because she felt the same. "We've got today." Even to her, as she said it, it sounded like a consolation prize.

Cole didn't take it that way. He walked over to her and took her hands in his. "Okay. Then let's pack in as much as we can in one day. It's not like we won't see each other again. You'll be back after the new year."

"Right. So let's not let it ruin our day! First stop... What haven't we done?"

"Sledding?"

"Fantastic! First, let's have breakfast."

Cole leaned closer until their foreheads nearly touched. "I like how you think!"

Together, they made omelets, home fries, and toast.

Afterward, Sophie put her hand on her stomach. "I'm stuffed. Now we've got to go do something active."

Cole stood and pointed to the door. "On to sledding."

They put on their snow gear and headed outside. Sophie dragged an old toboggan out of the garage.

While Cole pretended to tighten a lace on his boots, he said, "Sledding's okay, but you know what's even better?"

"No." Before she could turn back, a snowball struck her in the back. She raised an eyebrow and turned. "Oh, you are going to regret that."

He taunted her. "I'm scared already." While he reached down to make another snowball, he was struck in the arm. "What was that?"

She grinned. "High school girls' softball team." She pointed to herself with her thumbs. "Pitcher."

He stared for a moment. "Oh, crap."

"Oh, yeah. It's on!"

She was pummeling him with a barrage of snowballs when he suddenly ran toward her and tackled her, landing them both in a pile of snow. Then he mimicked her by pointing a thumb to his chest. "Football team." Holding a handful of snow, he offered her a choice. "This or a kiss."

"I don't know. That snow looks pretty good."

"Don't tempt me." He moved the handful of snow closer and closer.

Sophie squealed. "It's so cold out! What if our lips stick together!"

"I'm willing to risk it. Are you?" He moved the snow closer and let bits of it fall onto her neck.

"Okay! I'll take the kiss!"

Cole's lips touched hers, and she nearly forgot they were lying in the snow. Cole pulled away and searched Sophie's eyes. As their smiles faded, a car full of teenagers drove by, honking and whistling through open windows.

Cole laughed, and they both ran inside. After they'd stomped off all the snow and hung up their coats, mittens, scarves, and hats, they headed back to the kitchen for coffee.

Sophie's phone rang. Expecting her grandmother again, Sophie was surprised to see a strange number. Cole made coffee while she went into the living room and spoke on the phone. A few minutes later, she returned to the kitchen. "I can't believe it."

Cole raised his eyebrows and waited.

"It's a job interview. After the new year."

Cole's expression clouded over. "Where?"

Sophie knew where this was going, and she didn't want to answer. "In the city."

His eyes lost their warmth as he nodded. "You're not coming back."

"Well, no, that's not true."

"It is if you get the job."

"Well, yes, but what are the odds?"

"Good. Probably better than good."

Sophie wasn't sure what to say. If it wasn't this job, it could be another. "It was going to happen at some point. I can't afford not to work. I wouldn't feel right even if I could. I know it sounds stupid, but I want to make the world better, or at least my little corner of it."

Cole's eyes narrowed. "You're right. I get it. What I don't get is your eagerness to go back there to do it. It's not the same place that you left. Why go back?"

She felt as though she were being accused when she hadn't done anything wrong. "I could ask you a similar question. Why won't you go back? If every-body just gives up and runs away from trouble, where are we?"

"I didn't ruin my business or my neighborhood. Others did, and they seem to want it that way. So why not let them have it?"

For the first time, Sophie saw how bitter Cole truly was. "I get how you feel. It must've been awful to watch your store destroyed. But you can't be so cynical."

"Oh, I don't know. I think you underestimate me."

Sophie said softly, "But I feel like you're angry with me."

He looked into her eyes. "I'm not. I just hate to see you... go there."

"It's a few hours away."

"Five." He looked almost scornful. "It might as well be a whole world away. But it's not really the distance, is it? No matter how hard we try, we keep ending up here—so far apart philosophically that it's hopeless."

Sophie grimaced. "Relationships aren't philo-sophical."

Undaunted, Cole pressed on with his point. "You want to be part of a world I despise, and I will never go back to the city. So here we are, at an impasse."

Sophie searched Cole's eyes, wishing she could feel the connection they'd felt only minutes before, but she saw something else. "I didn't get it until now."

"Get what?"

"Something my grandmother told me."

"Look, nothing against Grandma Kate, but—"

"Forgiveness is a miracle you have the power to make happen."

"Okay, my turn. A stitch in time saves nine."

Sophie narrowed her eyes but refused to give up. "There's a lot of anger and bitter resentment out there. It can keep you from living your life."

"Tell that to the people who smashed in my windows and looted my store."

Sophie said, "But think of how sad it must be for them. They're imprisoned by their own rage."

"I don't know. The guys who beat the crap out of me didn't look so sad." Clenching his jaw, Cole looked away.

"I know it's hard. But I honestly believe that forgiveness will free you and make room for hope."

"Hope." Cole smiled bitterly. "The only hope I have is that your job interview goes well and you have a good life." He headed for the door.

Sophie followed. "Don't do that!"

"Do what?"

"Don't just dismiss me like that."

He turned back. "You're right. You deserve more. Look, we met one another in a sort of temporary environment. We were both taking a break from the world. But it's over. It's time for you to go back and for me to move on."

Sophie wanted to tell him that he could come with her, but she knew better than that.

"I'm sorry, Sophie." He kissed her on the forehead then left.

16

Cole wasn't home the next morning when Sophie locked the door to the cottage and headed for home. She supposed they had already said their goodbyes, but she hated the way they had left things. On the plus side, there was no doubt about whether it was over. She wouldn't have to waste time hoping for something that was never going to happen.

She drew in a deep breath and exhaled. This was not going to ruin her Christmas, because she wouldn't let it. In spite of the last-minute change in location, she was on her way home for the holidays. She was blessed to have a family like hers. Even her brother, who could be annoying, had her back when it counted. And this family knew how to do Christmas. They would go shopping, bake cookies, and eat popcorn while watching their favorite holiday movies together—like so many families.

Between Christmas and the New Year, she usually touched base with school friends. Until now, her biggest problem at holiday time had been too much delicious food. This year, as much as she tried to distract herself, Cole cropped up in her thoughts more often than she cared to admit.

Once home, when the excitement of arriving home to be with family died down, Sophie curled up with a book and a blanket on the window seat, but she couldn't seem to immerse herself in the story. She set the book on her lap and stared out the window.

Minutes later, her grandmother joined her. "I hear congratulations are in order."

It took Sophie a moment to realize what she was talking about. "Oh, the job interview. Thank you."

Her eyes narrowed as she studied Sophie. "It's just what you wanted."

Sophie wished she could lie and say yes, but she couldn't. "I thought so."

"What's changed?"

Sophie leveled a look at her grandmother. "I think you know the answer already."

Grandma Kate shook her head knowingly. "I told you to hang on to him."

"Yeah, but you didn't tell him. He let go."

"Oh. I have to say I'm surprised. He seemed awfully attentive."

"Yeah, I thought so." Sophie blew air through her lips. "I care about him, obviously... pathetically."

Grandma Kate shook her head. "Loving is never pathetic."

Sophie chuckled. "Oh, I don't know about that. Just hang around me for a while, and you'll see." Then her grandmother's choice of words dawned on her. "Hey, wait a minute. I didn't say *love*."

Grandma Kate smiled. "I know."

"Oh, come on, Grandma. Quit reading my mind."

"If it seems that way, it's only because you and I are alike in many ways. But the nice thing about life is that you have choices. Not only that, but you don't have to be stuck with your choices. You're allowed to change your mind and turn back."

Sophie knew exactly what was behind the kind but knowing look in her grandmother's eyes. "I can't. It's too late."

"Is it?" Without waiting for an answer, she stood. "You're a smart girl. You'll figure it out."

Uh, no, I'm not. And I probably won't. Sophie smiled, and her grandmother went to the kitchen.

Grandma Kate meant well, but she didn't get it.

This was not about changing minds. It was about two people whose lives just didn't fit together. Cole didn't know what he wanted, except that it wasn't Sophie. Or maybe it was, but he didn't want the rest that came with it. To be fair, Cole had lost a lot more than she had. He'd lost his business—his dream—and been assaulted in the process. She had just lost her job. It made sense that it would take him longer to rally, but how long would it take? Sophie couldn't wait around while Cole figured it out. For one thing, he didn't want her to. Yes, things happened in life that neither of them could control. All they could control was how they reacted. For Sophie, with one job interview already set up, she was ready to move forward. She had a goal and a plan of how to get there. Unfortunately, Cole had other plans.

Fishing had always been Cole's go-to coping strategy, but he couldn't even do that. There was too much time to think, and every thought led to Sophie. When he tried to imagine falling into step with her, he saw himself building a business, only to have it shattered again in an instant, just like the first. Cole liked things he could count on. When he got on a bike, he knew what would happen. He knew how to choose the right gear for the terrain. If something broke down, he knew how to fix it. That was the kind of life he wanted, with structure and predictability. That wasn't to say he didn't have a spirit of adventure. He liked taking risks on his bike, but even those risks were calculated. In business and finance, he didn't take risks.

That was the part of his reasoning where his thoughts always went back to Sophie. He had thrown away everything his common sense told him to be with her. He knew all the risks, but he couldn't stay away from her. He couldn't get their last time together out of his mind. He had hurt her and himself. He deserved what he got, but she didn't.

With any luck, Sophie would take her own advice and forgive him. That was some crazy theory her grandmother had. But it did get him thinking. Even if he could forgive his attackers and looters, he didn't see how that would free him. He wasn't even sure what he needed freeing from. He was a nice guy who generally did the right thing. He was nice to old ladies, like Sophie's grandmother, for example. He would have helped her across the street if the occasion arose. But his forgiveness wouldn't change the rioters' minds or their actions—unless they forgave too. Then he started to imagine what would happen if something like that caught on. If people forgave one another, they wouldn't have enough anger to fuel their destruction. *Then what would they do with all that leftover energy? Build a better world?*

Cole shook off the thought. *Back to real life.* He thought for a moment. Maybe it wasn't all that crazy. His own anger and resentment weren't making the rioters stop, and it certainly wasn't making his own life any better. Maybe he had come to a point at which he could let go of the past. He wasn't sure about being able to forgive, but setting his resentment aside was a step. He still couldn't see himself going back to his old neighborhood, but he'd made enough progress for one day.

While driving through Cedar Creek on his way home, Cole caught sight of an empty storefront. He'd noticed it before, but this time, he pulled over and parked. He walked over and looked through the window. The retail space was bigger than his store had been. He looked up and down the street. The location was good. The village got a lot of foot traffic, and the area was a tourist destination in the summer.

It would make a good home base for bike rentals and mountain bike tours. On a whim, Cole pulled out his phone and took a picture of the phone number on the real estate sign. It was a crazy idea, except that it wasn't.

He went back to his car and started to drive off, then he parked again and called the number on the sign. He shouldn't have been surprised that the real estate agent's office was three blocks away and she could meet him there in fifteen minutes. She showed him around the store. There was enough space for storage and a workshop in the back. The rent was low compared to what he had paid in the city. Of course, the foot traffic would be more seasonal here, but with the rent and added income from mountain bike tours in the summer, it could work.

Cole thanked the real estate agent and said he would be in touch after the holidays. He drove away, intending to set the idea aside until then. But once formed, the idea would not go away.

Forty miles down the highway, still musing about the storefront, Cole caught sight of the exit to Sophie's hometown. On an impulse, he took it. He pulled into the first gas station to refuel and rethink his new problem with impulse control—first the store and now this. He didn't know where she lived. All he knew was her cell number, but then he remembered something. When they'd exchanged numbers, she'd texted her contact card to him. He pulled out his phone and grinned. There it was—her home address. She might be all over the kitchen, but she hadn't updated her phone contact list in a couple of years. Sometimes he just loved technology.

Ten minutes later, he was at her front door. The door swung open.

"Kate. Hi."

"Cole. How are you? Come in."

"I was in the neighborhood." *Brilliant opener.* "I was hoping I might speak with Sophie."

She looked genuinely disappointed. "I'm so sorry. She's out."

Of course she is. What did you expect? He tried to look casual, as though it barely mattered. "Oh, okay. As I said, I was in the area. I'm on my way home for Christmas, and I thought I'd stop by."

"Oh, that's so nice! I'll tell her you stopped by. Why don't you let me make you some coffee for the road? It'll just take a minute."

"Thanks, that's so nice, but I'm good. I've got a travel mug in the car." If she looked any kinder or more sympathetic, he might slip and show his true feelings.

"She'll be disappointed that she missed you."

He shrugged. "No worries. Merry Christmas."

"You too, Cole." She smiled warmly and stood at the door until he was inside his car. He drove off and spent the next twenty minutes of his trip wondering why he'd even done that. But the truth was, he knew.

17

When Sophie got home, Grandma Kate pulled her aside. "Your hot next-door neighbor stopped by."

"Grandma!"

"What? He's good-looking."

Sophie couldn't argue with that. "What did he say?"

"He didn't."

Dismayed, Sophie shook her head. "He came all this way and didn't even leave a message?"

Grandma Kate sat at the kitchen table and gestured for Sophie to join her. "No, but I imagine he thought it would be awkward to confess his love to your grandmother, so he decided to wait."

Despite Grandma Kate's amusement, Sophie couldn't even smile. This was too unexpected, and she didn't want to jump to conclusions, unlike her grandmother.

"Why don't you text him?"

It wasn't a bad idea, but she shook her head. "He's driving. I wouldn't want to distract him." But she hadn't ruled out texting him later, when she knew he would be home. She shut her eyes and rubbed her forehead for a moment. "Maybe he just stopped by to torture me by making me wonder like this."

"No. He wanted to see you. He tried to look like he wasn't disappointed, but I saw through that act."

Sophie let out a miserable sigh. "I was sure it was over. I was getting used to the idea. It still hurt, but at least I'd stopped hoping." She looked up and exhaled. "I wish I could be more like you."

Her grandmother let out a laugh. "Oh, believe me, that's not something to wish for."

"But, Grandma, you're so strong and independent. Just when I think I can take charge of my life and be happy alone, some guy comes along and messes everything up."

Grandma Kate took her granddaughter's hands in hers. "Taking charge of your life doesn't mean you have to be alone."

"But you've lived alone, and you look way happier than I do."

Grandma Kate gazed at Sophie with a wistful

smile. "I've had the great love of my life. I haven't met anyone like him, and I don't expect to. So I'm content with my life and my memories." She let her thoughts stray for a moment then asked, "So tell me something. Do you love him?"

Sophie shrugged. "I don't know. How do you know?"

"You'll figure it out."

Sophie shook her head. "I don't think I want to know—unless there's a chance. How can I know if we've barely just met?"

"I don't have the answer to that. I do know that love comes to people in different ways. Sometimes it quietly creeps up over time, until one day it's just there. Other times, like with your grandfather, it was practically instant. I met him, and I knew he was the one."

"Grandma, that's so romantic!"

"Not really. I was overwhelmed with emotion, and he was this big strapping guy who was painfully shy. I didn't find out until much later that he felt the same way. It took him months to muster the courage to ask me out."

"Oh, that's so sweet."

"Looking back, yes, it was. But, as you know, love can also make you unsure of yourself and entirely miserable. I still remember that feeling."

Sophie nodded with sudden realization. "Then, by that definition, I must be in love!" She laughed, then her eyes filled with tears.

Grandma Kate sighed. "Only you know if Cole is the one. All I know is that love is a gift. If you're lucky enough to find it, fight for it, keep it, and treasure it."

With furrowed eyebrows, Sophie nodded slowly.

Cole chided himself the entire way home. He had no one to blame but himself. He had acted on impulse without thinking it through. Now the worst had happened. She wasn't at home, but by now, he was sure she'd been told. Grandma Kate wouldn't forget about that. Sophie wouldn't laugh at him. She was too kind for that. No, she would just feel sorry for him, and that felt even worse.

Cole arrived home and went through the motions of looking happy. When evening came and everyone settled down to watch a holiday movie, Cole was relieved. His parents were on the opposite side of the room, while his brother's attention was fully engaged by his wife and six-year-old daughter. Cole could finally wallow in self-pity without anyone noticing. After reliving in his mind the humiliation of standing at Sophie's door, unable to offer a logical reason for his presence, he went through the sequence leading to his romantic demise. There were sparks. There had always been sparks. And they'd had fun together, had interesting talks, and laughed at the same things. In almost every way, it was an ideal romance. But it took more than that to build a lasting relationship. And that was where it all fell apart.

Whoever said love conquered all? By now, thoroughly bored with the movie, Cole looked it up on his phone. *Virgil?* He blew air through his lips, prompting little Peyton to turn around and, from her seat on the floor in front of the TV, give him a stern warning look. He lifted an eyebrow then crossed his eyes, proving himself the less mature of the two. But she turned back to the TV, so he counted that as a win.

Back to Virgil. Life was simpler then. There were no electric cars. Wheels were chiseled out of stone. *Maybe that was the Flintstones. Same thing.* The point was, twenty-first-century life wasn't easy. You couldn't just fall in love and build a life around that. There were more important things to consider, like jobs and lifestyles—and compatible hobbies. *When did love fall by the wayside?*

Cole stood and caught another chastising look from Peyton, the little darling, and went to his room. Far from the boyish digs of his youth, his room had been turned into a craft room, where half-finished projects were strewn about an L-shaped arrangement of folding tables holding a sewing machine. Assorted plastic tubs of God knew what were stacked precariously and placed around the perimeter. At least his mother had left enough floor space for him to pace undisturbed.

He loved Sophie. He supposed he had known it, but he just hadn't put it into words. Now, as he said those three words, it became truth, clear and indisputable. He loved Sophie. He said it a few more times to himself, almost as though he were trying on a garment to see how it fit. He decided to keep it.

His love for Sophie cast a new light on the rest of his life. While he didn't disagree with the concept of forgiveness, he hadn't set out to apply it to himself. But as his love for Sophie grew, his desire to be with her overshadowed the emotions that, since the riot, had driven his actions and thoughts. While he still wished none of it had ever happened, he had been lucky enough to recover from his injuries with no lasting effects. Starting over from scratch wasn't something he relished. Still, he would always look back fondly on how he had built a business and become part of a neighborhood community. If he did it once, he could do it again.

Some might say that the looters and rioters won

in the end, but Cole knew better. There were two types of people in the world—builders and destroyers. Cole was one of the builders. There would always be people hell-bent on destroying. He would leave it to those who enjoyed studying such things to explain why. People had all kinds of reasons for anger, most likely well-grounded. But people had choices. They could let anger control them, or they could forgive.

Cole loved Sophie too much to waste any more time on the people who'd hurt him. Maybe Virgil was right, and love did conquer all. Cole left the past in the past and looked toward his future. That was something he had the power to build.

Suddenly, Cole felt hope! *Score one for Grandma Kate.* Letting go of the past was a liberating sensation. The clouds parted, releasing the sun to shine its warmth over the land. Life was good. All he wanted was a future with Sophie.

Then Cole's hope fell to the floor with a thud. Sophie didn't want him, at least not enough. In her eyes, theirs was just another relationship that hadn't worked out.

18

Sophie continued to scour the job market. There wasn't a lot, but she found two more jobs to apply for. At this time of year, that seemed good. By now, everyone was on vacation, but she hoped she could hit the ground running in the new year.

Matt walked past her room and found her staring blankly at her computer. "Man, Sophie, give it a rest. It's Christmas. Relax and enjoy it. You've got plenty of time to work your butt off later."

She leaned back with a sigh. "I know. I've been scrolling through the same listings thinking something might change."

Matt narrowed his eyes. "I mean, it's paraphrased, but isn't that the definition of insanity?"

Sophie tilted her head. "Close enough."

Matt frowned. "Maybe I'm the insane one. I can't

believe I'm going to say this, but let's go shopping. We could make a quick run through the mall and then settle onto some barstools for drinks."

Sophie stared at her brother for a couple of moments. "That's actually not a bad idea."

"You don't have to say it. I know you're impressed."

Sophie grinned. "Something like that. I'll meet you downstairs in ten minutes."

A few hours later, while sipping spiked eggnog at a mall restaurant bar, Sophie had what she tried to describe as a road-to-Damascus experience, but three drinks into their talk, she couldn't quite get the words out. "Road to Damocles? No, that's not it."

Through his laughter, Matt said, "I'm pretty sure that's a sword. But I get what Cole sees in you. You're a really cheap date."

Sophie frowned into her drink. "I love him."

Matt's eyebrows drew together while his lips spread into a smile. "You poor thing."

"I am poor—because I don't have a job. I should go home and look through the listings again."

Matt stood. "I'm on board with the first part."

As they made their way to the exit, Sophie said, "Which part? The part where I love him?"

"Sure." Matt opened the door.

"But that ship has sailed." She sighed. "I love that carol."

She'd lost Matt. "The *I love him* carol?"

She sat down in the car and began singing. "I saw three ships come..." She paused and shut her eyes, thinking hard. "I saw three ships come..."

Matt took pity and joined in while nodding encouragingly. "Sailing in on Christmas Day, on Christmas Day..." They spent the ten-minute drive home singing multiple verses, none of which could be found in *The Oxford Book of Carols*.

They arrived home to find Grandma Kate supervising a rambunctious game of pin the tail on the reindeer. An hour later, having sufficiently worn out the children and some of the adults, everyone gathered in the family room with pillows, blankets, and flannel pajamas for a Christmas movie night. While Sophie sipped coffee and helped Grandma Kate make popcorn, the two of them talked.

Sophie said, "I did what you suggested."

"Which suggestion was that?"

"Forgiving. And it's worked, sort of."

"That doesn't sound like a glowing endorsement."

"Well, it's worked for my professional life, but my personal life kind of got lost in the bargain."

Her grandmother shrugged. "Oh, well, that's easily solved."

"Is it?" Sophie was doubtful.

"Someone needs to pull over and make a U-turn —or at least look at a map and find an alternate route."

Sophie sighed. "If only it were that easy."

Her grandmother said, "Life can be hard sometimes. This isn't one of those times. You love him. He loves you. Make it happen."

Sophie wished she could, but it was too late. She wasn't even sure if Cole's feelings were as serious as hers. She supposed she could drive for an hour to his house and throw herself at him. The idea had its merits, but then it could easily go sideways and ruin her Christmas by leaving her feeling rejected and miserable. That sort of humiliation could etch its impression into not only her memory but also her soul and ruin Christmas for the rest of her life. No, that option was out, leaving... no more options. It was over.

Although sympathetic, Grandma Kate was too busy pouring popcorn into bowls to have time for Sophie's sorry love life. So Sophie sucked it up and distributed bowls of popcorn, then she sat down with a sigh.

A half hour into the movie, Grandma Kate tapped Sophie's shoulder and signaled for her to follow. They sat at the kitchen table, then Grandma Kate pulled out her phone and set it down on the table. "I've been texting a couple of friends in Cedar Creek."

"Oh, that's nice."

"Well, I think it could be, or at least it's worth thinking about."

"Okay."

Grandma Kate appeared to think Sophie should know what she was talking about. Sophie didn't, but Grandma Kate wasn't getting any younger. Maybe she had reached a point where she wouldn't make sense all the time. Who was Sophie to judge?

"What if you found a job in Cedar Creek?"

Sophie shrugged. "I don't know. I guess I just always saw myself going back to the city. That's what I always wanted, and I liked it."

Grandma Kate had this gaze that bored through a person when she wanted the truth. Sophie had flashbacks to her childhood, when she had stolen a cookie from the cooling rack and smeared melted chocolate chips on her cheek. Grandma Kate always knew.

"Is it still what you want?" Grandma Kate asked.

"I don't know. Is this a trick question?"

"No, but it's tricky. My friend Lorna's daughter is about to give birth. If I'm not mistaken, this will be number three."

"Oh, sounds busy." Sophie seemed to recall meeting Lorna's daughter. She was Sophie's age and expecting her third child. Was this another reminder that Sophie was losing the biological race?

"I just exchanged a few texts with Lorna, and Mallory—that's Lorna's daughter—has her hands full. She's decided not to go back."

"Go back where?"

"To work. She works for the police department as a dispatcher."

"Oh."

"She told them two weeks ago that she's leaving, and her due date is in a week. They're desperate to find someone to replace her. She said Mallory's almost certain they'd take you on temporarily. If that worked out, it could turn into full-time."

"In Cedar Creek?" The news caught Sophie by surprise. She wasn't sure what to make of it.

"Oh, I almost forgot to mention that Lorna saw Cole—"

"Wait. She knows Cole?"

"No, but it's a small town. A hot guy like that

doesn't wander around without someone finding out who he is."

"That's a little disconcerting."

Grandma Kate's eyes twinkled. "In a comforting way."

Sophie wrinkled her brow. "Yeah, whatever."

"My point is—pay attention—your Cole has his eye on an empty storefront."

Sophie stared at her grandmother. "He's staying in Cedar Creek?"

"Well, I don't know that for sure, but he seems to be considering it."

"Grandma, you have been busy!"

Her grandmother grinned. "I'm not much of a knitter, so it helps pass the time. You know, you ought to try texting."

"Okay, Grandma, you lost me."

"If your guy went to the trouble to stop by to see you, the least you could do is reach out."

"You mean Cole? You want me to text him?"

With a mischievous look, Grandma Kate said, "Well, it doesn't much matter what I want, but it might matter to him." She stood. "While you do that, I've got a movie to watch."

19

Cole's phone dinged with a text, which earned him a chastising look from Peyton. He surreptitiously pointed to his brother, her father, beside him as though he'd been the culprit. She turned her scowl to her father while Cole slipped out of the room.

In the dim light of the dining room, Cole sat down to study Sophie's text message: *You stopped by my house.*

Cole answered: *Yes.*

Before he could type out an explanation, she replied: *?*

Cursing his slow thumb-typing skill, Cole dictated. "We need to talk."

Sophie: *We need to balk?*

Cole: *Not balk. Talk.*

Sophie: *Okay. Call me.*

Peyton was on her way back from the bathroom when she spied him at the dining room table. "Uncle Cole! No phones at the table. Mommy said."

"I'm allowed. Mommy said."

She frowned in confused disbelief.

Cole widened his eyes and nodded confidently. "Go ask her."

Still confused, she left.

Sophie: *Hello? Did you still want to talk?*

Cole's niece returned with her mother in tow. "Peyton said you needed to talk to me."

He looked from Peyton to her mother. "No, I didn't." Forgetting his phone mic was on, he inadvertently texted those same words to Sophie.

Sophie: *???*

Cole glanced from his phone to his sister-in-law, then he held up his phone. "I was on the phone and... never mind. It was a misunderstanding."

Perceiving a teachable moment, Peyton's mother knelt down to Peyton's eye level. "Peyton? Tell Mommy what happened."

Peyton lifted her chin. "Uncle Cole had his phone at the dinner table."

"Yes, but Uncle Cole is a grown-up."

"So is Daddy, but you always tell him to get off the damn phone."

Her mother's forced smile revealed a twinge of

embarrassment. "Yes, but we're not in charge of Uncle Cole."

Peyton nodded with clear understanding. "But we're still in charge of Daddy, right?"

Cole looked back at his phone.

Sophie: *Okay. I guess you've changed your mind.*

Cole said, "No!"

Peyton and her mother both turned to Cole with their jaws dropped.

"Excuse me," Cole said and left the room. He stepped into the mudroom, where the dog looked up from a nap, looking sympathetic as Cole hastily dialed the phone. "Sophie, I'm sorry about the texts. There's a lot going on here."

"Okay." She didn't sound okay, but at least she was talking.

"I need to talk to you."

"That's what we're doing."

"In person. Are you busy?"

"It's Christmas Eve."

"I know, but it's important."

Sophie said, "We're getting ready to leave for a midnight Christmas Eve service."

"Where's your church?"

Sophie told him, and he said, "I'll meet you there."

"You want to talk during the service?"

"No, after. I'll meet you outside."

"But you live—"

"An hour away. I can drive it."

There was a long pause, then Sophie sighed. "Okay."

A light snow drifted downward as Sophie walked out of the midnight church service. On the sidewalk ahead, Cole stood waiting for her.

Matt leaned over and muttered, "If things go south, you can call me, and I'll pick you up."

Grandma Kate hooked her arm with Matt's. "That's enough, Matt. Help an elderly lady walk to the car."

Matt looked sideways at her. "If I could find an elderly lady, I would."

Sophie's mother gave her shoulder a squeeze as she and her father walked on toward the car with the others, leaving Sophie and Cole on the sidewalk.

People walked past on the way to their cars, some smiling, some laughing as Christmas joy filled the air. All Sophie felt was the heartache she'd hidden since she arrived home.

"Sophie."

"Hi, Cole." Sophie wasn't sure if her heart was sinking or her stomach was churning.

The parking lot emptied out, and the overhead lights caught flakes of sparkling snow as it fell to the ground.

Cole said, "I've been thinking."

Sophie waited.

His mouth spread into a smile. "About something your grandmother said."

Weary from heartache, Sophie could barely react. "So you called me to talk about Grandma Kate?"

Cole's eyes shone as he gazed into her eyes. "She was right."

Confused, Sophie said softly, "She's always right."

"I believe it." The hush of falling snow settled upon them. "The thing is, once I let go of the past, everything looked so clear."

"I'm glad that you're happy." *So that's what he called me here for.* She had tried to prepare herself for the inevitable letdown, but now that it was here, it hurt just the same. She had been foolish to hope.

Cole took a step closer. "What I saw clearly was you. You are all that matters to me—more than where I work or what might happen."

She looked into his eyes, afraid to trust what she saw there.

"The thing is, Sophie, I love you."

"Cole—"

"No, don't say it. I know that we've had disagreements, but it's all been a little overwhelming, and then I met you, and it happened so fast—"

She put her fingertips to his mouth. "Stop talking. I love you."

For a moment, he stared at her, looking stunned. His lips parted. "I'll go wherever you want—to the city, the country—I just want you."

Sophie willed herself not to cry. "I know."

She'd barely gotten the words out when Cole took her face in his hands and kissed her. A tear trailed down her cheek.

20

Six Weeks Later

On a brisk afternoon, Sophie walked out the door of the Cedar Creek police station, where she worked as a dispatcher, then walked two blocks to an empty storefront. Looking up at the sign that read Cole's Bikes and Tours, she smiled and decided she would never get tired of seeing that. She stepped inside and walked past a paint-splattered ladder and drop cloth on her way to the back room to change into her work clothes. They'd been working for weeks to renovate Cole's new store. He planned to sell, rent, and repair bikes and give mountain bike tours to weekenders. In two more weeks, he would be ready to open.

Sophie called out, "How's it coming?"

Cole called out from the back room, "Good. How

was work?"

Unwrapping her scarf, she said, "There's a lot to be said for small-town life. But today was especially quiet—not that I'm complaining." She stopped in the doorway, and her face lit up.

Looking up with a smile, Cole finished lighting two candles on a folding card table covered with a linen tablecloth and flowers. "Maybe it's slow because it's Valentine's Day." He pulled out a chair for her.

"Thank you." Her eyes shone as she sat down and looked up at him.

Cole's mouth turned up at the corner as he poured two glasses of champagne and handed one to Sophie.

She lifted her glass and toasted, "Here's to building new ventures."

"Funny you should mention that. I've got another idea for a new venture."

"Oh?" They hadn't gotten their current one off the ground yet, but she didn't want to spoil his enthusiasm. "What is it?"

"Us." Cole dropped to one knee. Pulling a ring from his pocket, he said, "Sophie, I love you. Will you marry me?"

Amid boxes of bikes and piles of unassembled display shelving, Sophie said, "Yes."

THANK YOU!

Thank you, reader. With so many options, I appreciate your choosing my book to read. Your opinion matters, so please consider sharing a review to help other readers.

BOOK NEWS

Would you like to know when the next book comes out? Click below to sign up for the J.L. Jarvis Journal and get book news, free books, and exclusive content delivered monthly.

news.jljarvis.com

ACKNOWLEDGMENTS

Editing by Red Adept Editing
redadeptediting.com

ABOUT THE AUTHOR

J.L. Jarvis is a left-handed opera singer/teacher/lawyer who writes books. She received her undergraduate training from the University of Illinois at Urbana-Champaign and a doctorate from the University of Houston. She now lives and writes in upstate New York.

Sign up to be notified of book releases and related news:
news.jljarvis.com

Email JL at:
writer@jljarvis.com

Follow JL online at:
jljarvis.com

facebook.com/jljarvis1writer

twitter.com/JLJarvis_writer

instagram.com/jljarvis.writer

bookbub.com/authors/j-l-jarvis

pinterest.com/jljarviswriter

goodreads.com/5106618.J_L_Jarvis

amazon.com/author/B005G0M2Z0

youtube.com/UC7kodjlaG-VcSZWhuYUUl_Q

Made in the USA
Las Vegas, NV
07 September 2021